Adam Brown, the Merchant

Horace Smith

Contents

ADAM BROWN, THE MERCHANT

BY

Horace Smith

ADAM BROWN.

CHAPTER I.

As the imagination has a larger grasp than the senses, there may be some truth in the dictum that the unknown always appears magnificent; but this position must be restricted to a certain class of aggrandizing processes. When their curiosity is baffled, people are apt to be rather indignant than magnifying, to make their ignorance an excuse for their ill-nature, and to pronounce all those impulses mean or unworthy which they cannot immediately and clearly fathom,—an ungenerous tendency which received abundant illustration in the case of Allan Latimer. High as his character stood, unexceptionable as had been his whole career since his first settlement at Woodcote, there were not wanting tattlers to make the significant remark that he could not have gone away so suddenly for nothing, and to insinuate that, if there had been a good reason for his flight, it would undoubtedly have been brought forward by his family. Availing themselves of this logical deduction, and assuming the fact of a bad reason, since they had not heard a good one, the gossips set to work to ferret out what it was, each assigning his own theory, his own selected folly or misdemeanor, as the most plausible solution of the mystery. Let it be recorded, however, to the credit of the village, that others, more charitable and just in their conclusions, felt and expressed their confidence in Allan's honour and good conduct, and rebuked the whisperers of these injurious surmises.

Though no one could be more surprised and distressed at his unaccountable departure than his mother, not for a single moment was her mind clouded by any misgiving as to its causes. When some of her prying neighbours kindly intimated their hope that he had not got into any scrape, or involved himself in any unpleasant embarrassments—phrases rather suggested by their curiosity than their sympathy—she replied with a placid smile, "I am as much in the dark as yourself, touching the real motives which have taken him from home for a short time, for he promises an early return; but I know my dear boy well; I know the principles in which he has been educated, and, whatever may have been his motives, I have implicit confidence in their propriety. Ours, thank God, has been a household of love; we have ever put trust in one another, and I have no fear that anything can have occurred to disturb it, or that this our first separation will be of long continuance. At times Allan may be a little hasty and impetuous, but his heart is in the right place, and, whatever may be his actions, depend upon it he will be well able to justify them when he comes back among us. Dear boy! blessings upon him wherever he may be!"

Accurately to describe the feelings of Matilda Molloy, when she learnt the flight of Allan would require a larger space than we can at present devote to the analysis. Although she could lay the flattering unction to her soul, that, as she had merely acted in obedience to her father's wishes, her conduct was filially meritorious, in the same degree that it might be deemed morally censurable, she could not help bitterly reproaching herself for the part she had acted. And yet, perhaps, it was the failure rather than the attempt that mortified and vexed her. Even while condemning herself, however, she hated Allan more bitterly than she had ever liked him, because her aversion was not in proportion to her previous predilection, but to her present disappointment.

It is well known that we generally dislike those whom we have injured, but there is a class towards whom we cherish a still more intense repugnance,—those whom we have sought to injure or cajole, and have been baffled in our attempt, within which category Allan might now be placed. Yet Matilda, though a bold and forward girl, and rather unscrupulous where her prospects of an advantageous marriage were at stake, was not without a sense of right and wrong, which, in the present instance, maintained an occasional and harassing struggle with her wounded self-love and frustrated hopes, Time and reflection, where the mind is not thoroughly demoralized, generally mitigate our evil tendencies and fortify our good ones; and so it proved with Matilda, who, as her first anger and mortification gave way to a calmer retrospect of her recent conduct, found it much more easy to forgive Allan than herself.

As to Ellen, she had become quite an altered girl since the mutual confession of love and solemn betrothal with Walter. The long and anxious concealment which had "preyed on her damask cheek," the doubts and fears and humiliating self-reproaches which had depressed her spirits and undermined her health, were rapidly dissipated by the cheering certainty that her affection was deeply, sincerely, fervently reciprocated. True, the difficulties that opposed their immediate union were as formidable as ever; but she could talk about that union with him to whom she had given her whole heart,—she could look forward to a future day-spring of happiness, however remote; and her hope had not yet been deferred long enough to make her heart sick. On the contrary, it fed upon that hope, and seemed to require no other sustenance to ensure its present felicity.

A girl feels such an exhilaration, such a sweetness, in possessing the affections of one whose preference exalts her in her own regard, and there is such a sublimising buoyancy in the young soul where this delightful sensation is experienced for the first time! Ellen's improved health and cheer of mind might almost have justified the averment of the French author, that the true honeymoon is that which precedes marriage, even where this antepast becomes extended over several months. Her guitar, and her singing, and all her former recreations were resumed, while frequent walks and an interchange of entire confidence with her lover exercised an equally beneficial influence in restoring the roses to her cheek and a blissful serenity to her bosom. Both being equally averse from clandestine proceedings of any sort, both willing, and indeed determined, to defer their marriage until some change of circumstances should give it the warranty of prudence, Walter determined to seek some occupation that might hold out to him a prospect, however distant, of being enabled to support a wife, provided that object could be accomplished without separating himself from his mother, who had now double need of his society and solace.

"My dear boy!" said Mrs. Latimer, when her son imparted his secret to her, and implored her sanction of the conditional arrangement he had made, "you are sure of my assent to anything that may promote your happiness; and as Ellen is a very good girl, gentle and kind, and affectionate like yourself, I dare say she will make an excellent wife; but still, dear Walter, I cannot help thinking you might have done better for yourself."

"Not in personal recommendations, mother; and as to ambitious views, they are foreign to ray nature; I never indulged any aspiring thoughts."

"Nor I either: Heaven knows I have no right. It becomes me to be lowly, and humble, and unpresuming, both as regards myself and my family,—and I trust I am so. I would not look too high for you; quite the contrary: but you must confess that Captain Molloy's family, on various accounts, is not the most desirable one in the world to be connected with. Now, if you could only have found a girl equal in every respect to Ellen, only with a few trifling additions, such as superior birth, a handsome fortune, and powerful relations, I can't help thinking, somehow, that it might have been preferable."

"Very possibly," smiled Walter; "but would such a girl have me? What should I have to offer in return for such accumulated advantages?"

"Yourself, dear Walter," replied the mother, gazing on him with a proud and affectionate look; "as good and as true a man as ever blessed a woman with his love. **Have** you! Why, a princess, a queen might be proud to have you."

"But as I don't mean to propose either to a queen or a princess, and have plighted my troth to dear Ellen, I trust you will approve my choice."

"Ay, that I will, with all my heart and soul, if it will contribute to your peace of mind. And as to your looking out for some employment that may place you in a situation to marry sooner and with greater comfort, never mind me, dear Walter, if you can find anything at a distance. Allan, I dare say, will soon return, and, if not, I don't mind being alone, not in the least. Only let me hear that you are getting on and doing well; I shall not require anything else. Besides, Ellen will be always here, and I shall look upon her now as my intended daughter-in-law, so that I shan't be dull."

"No, no, mother!" said Walter, tenderly embracing her; "I should be the most ungrateful wretch in the world if I loved anybody half so well as you. I will not consult my own gratification at your expense, depend on't; indeed, I don't think I could feel any pleasure if I were to be separated from you."

"Bless you, my kind-hearted boy! I do not think you could. Ah! if our good friend Mr. Brown now would do something for you! Don't you think you had better inform him how matters stand between you and Ellen?"

"No, indeed; he was so cross and so rude the last time I called, that I have no wish to subject myself to a renewal of such treatment."

"Leave it then to me—I know how to manage him; and it is quite right that he should be apprized of your engagement."

Ellen's first communication was made to her sister, who received it without surprise, for the marked improvement in her spirits and health had already revealed her secret. Matilda was sincerely attached to her sister, and had a strong feeling that a pretty girl like Ellen would be throwing herself away to marry a pauper, as she called Walter; under the influence of which double impression, she strenuously urged her to hold herself disengaged, and to take the chance of a visit to Cheltenham during the season, of which some hopes had been thrown out to them by the Captain. Finding her however inflexible in holding herself betrothed, though quite willing to pledge herself against any rash precipitation, and even to protract their marriage for years, should circumstances render it advisable, she consented, at Ellen's request, who felt herself unequal to the task, to impart the state of her affections and the fact of her betrothal to her father.

"Ho! by the powers! it's that way the wind blows, is it?" exclaimed the Captain. "Well,' Tilda dear, if we can't secure that runaway Shabberoon Allan for you, it will be no bad spec to hook the brother for Nell. Walter's a nice young chap; but in his present plight, which is poor enough, and will be still worse when the old woman hops the twig, we mustn't hear of any marrying, nor must a syllable be said upon the subject to old Brown."

"There I quite agree with you. It would offend him beyond measure; for he never loses an opportunity of uttering angry denunciations against improvident marriages and love engagements."

"Lookye, 'Tilda! this must be our course. By hook or by crook, Walter must succeed to his brother's place in the favour of old Brown, who has nobody else to whom he can leave his money; and to succeed in this object, we must take care to set him against Allan by every means in our power."

"That has been done pretty well already, for the old gentlemen t' other day desired me not to trouble my head about such a runaway, adding that he thought his behaviour towards me had been very scandalous."

"If we keep up that cry by running him down upon all occasions, and puffing Walter, my word for it he will soon be taken into favour, and stand in Allan's shoes; for the old fellow can't do without some one to toddle about and play billiards with him."

"And if he adopts Walter, he may probably make a settlement upon him immediately, and allow him to marry Ellen."

"And then the old curmudgeon may die as soon as he pleases. By the bye, he seems breaking already, and Walter will have the Manor-House estate and all the money besides, and Walter is a good-tempered-soft Tommy of a fellow, who will bleed freely, and put his hand to an acceptance now and then,—he couldn't do less for his own daddy-in-law: and then,' Tilda dear,—*by* the powers!—won't we make the kites fly, and rig ourselves out as fine as five horses, and cut a dash among the nabobs at Cheltenham, or perhaps astonish the natives at London, and pick up a rich husband for you as well as Nell!" Delighted with the vision he had thus conjured up, the Captain snapped his fingers, and joyously exclaimed, "Hurrah, then, girl, for Nell and Walter, and a winding-sheet for the old hunks as soon as he likes, that is to say, after he has settled everything upon my future son-in-law!"

At the recommendation of Captain Molloy, the force of whose arguments she immediately recognised, Mrs. Latimer was induced to abandon her intention of communicating to Mr. Brown the engagement into which her son had entered, willingly lending herself to the hope that, if Allan were finally to lose his favour, Walter might succeed to it, for she well knew that each would be ever ready to share his good fortune with the other. Adam Brown, in the mean while, the disposal of whose favour, fortune, and estate his neighbours were thus kindly anticipating, was in no very enviable state of mind. His health, as the Captain had truly stated, was again beginning to give way, and his temper, aggravated by the flight and unaccountable conduct of Allan Latimer, which was every day represented to him in a more unfavourable light, became at times exceedingly irritable. Inoccupation, and the want of a companion, added to his annoyances, under which circumstances he was glad to snatch at a change of locality, however short, and the prospect of a new visiting acquaintance, however remote, by going to see a Mr. Tomlinson, a brother merchant, whom he had formerly known at Smyrna, and who, having also retired from business, had purchased a house about fourteen miles from Woodcote, on the banks of the Severn. Wishing to give his old friend an agreeable surprise, he would not announce his intention by letter, but set off in the carriage, having first consulted a map of the county, and given the deaf coachman special instructions as to the road he was to take.

"Tomlinson's a good little fellow!" soliloquised the merchant, rubbing his hands in anticipation of a pleasant and a visitable neighbour—"very different from that daughter-pecked old fool Gregory Giblet—what's his other name? never mind, I forget his *alias. There's* an upstart! *there's* a jackass on his hind legs! *there's* a beggar on horseback! Talked of ducking me in the pond, didn't they? wish they had—wish they had smothered me in the mud: I'd have trounced them for it! Shan't be happy till I've had that jackadandy son of his tarred and feathered. Little Tomlinson's quite a different chap: proud of being a merchant and making his own money. Not much to brag of, though, in his case. Had a father before him—ready-made business—nothing to do but to follow his nose, and that's not very difficult, for it's a precious long one,—points out the way like a finger-post. No, no; little Tomlinson didn't run away from Woodcote with only seven and nine-pence in his pocket, ha! ha!"—Testifying his pleasure at this reminiscence by three triumphant raps of the cane on the bottom of the carriage, he beguiled the remainder of the drive by anticipating the surprise of his old friend at his unexpected appearance, and by devising schemes for exchanging visits of a week's continuance at each other's houses, that they might relieve their present *ennui* by talking over old days. At the time when he calculated they ought to have reached their destination, he desired John Trotman to make inquiries as to the direction of the house, and gave way to a burst of ill-temper when apprised that they had made an unnecessary détour of nearly three miles.

"Knew it all along," observed John Trotman very quietly and respectfully.

"Then, why the devil didn't you tell me?" demanded Brown angrily.

"Told you so twice before we started," was the reply: "seldom repeat the same thing twice, never three times." So saying, he made a motion with his finger to the deaf coachman, who turned round the carriage, and mended his pace that he might recover the ground they had lost. John was quite correct in his assertion. He never made inquiries, for that would imply talking, but he had a quick, almost an instinctive perception of bearings and localities, and he had twice set his master right when he heard him giving instructions to the coachman. Brown, however, whose active mind made him a regular factotum, and who believed that few people could know better than himself, petulantly overruled his objections, desiring the coachman to mind his master, and not attend to that stupid fellow. Most servants thus rudely reprimanded, would have exhibited a little triumph at the proof of their own superior sagacity; but, whatever John might feel on the occasion, his manner was as respectful, his look as phlegmatic and imperturbable as ever.

Reaching the house at length, and conning over the introductory speech with which he meant to mystify his old friend,—for Adam, even in his peevish moods, loved a little bit of waggery,—it would be difficult to describe his angry disappointment when he learnt from the servants that their master had left home on the previous day for Cheltenham, to which place he had resorted on account of the illness of his wife. "Just like my infernal luck!" he ejaculated, with something very like an oath. But it serves him right—perfectly right; and me too, for coming without writing. What *could* he expect? wives are always ill—as well marry a hospital! Never die though—know better—live to plague their husbands. Well, thank God! I never married—not such an ass."

As the horses could not set off upon their return until they had rested and baited, and there was no inn in the immediate vicinity, Brown willingly accepted the housekeeper's invitation that he should alight and partake such refreshment as the larder offered, while the horses were put up for an hour or two in the stable. Gratified as he was by this hospitable proposal, it did not soothe his bitter disappointment at the absence of little Tomlinson, the master of the mansion. Unluckily, too, he was exceedingly hungry,—the meal thus hastily and extemporaneously administered did not please his palate,—he was bored to death by having nothing to do,—and the evening had already set in before the coachman reported his horses to be in a fit condition for commencing their return home. Had it not been the fall moon, Brown, who was exceedingly averse from running any unnecessary risks, would have preferred sleeping at the first decent inn they might encounter; but, emboldened by the lightness of the night, and being moreover assured that the return by the direct road would hardly exceed thirteen miles, he gave most minute instructions to the coachman, and the carriage at length drove off.

There is no contending against fate: the journey was doomed to be disastrous in its end, as it had been inauspicious in its commencement. Owing to his deafness, the coachman misapprehended his instructions, again took a wrong road, and, in turning the carriage round to repair his error, upset it in a ditch concealed by shrubs and brambles. Quickly climbing to the upper side of the vehicle, John opened the door and helped his master to alight, pronouncing, in an interrogative tone, the single word "hurt?"

"Not in the least," was the reply: "that stupid fellow must have practised over-turning carriages,—taken lessons in the art,—or he never could have done it so gently. I hope he has not broken more than three or four of his own bones."

"Who could have ever guessed of this here kiver'd ditch?" growled the coach-man, struggling out of the bushes into which he had been thrown.

"Who could ever dream that I should be such a fool as to live in the country?" cried his master peevishly. "No dykes or ditches in London, except Fleet Ditch, and that's covered over—but not made into a trap with briers and leaves. Better live among the savages. Much better roads in Otaheite:—never hear of a carriage being upset in the deserts of Arabia. No house near us, of course, and the night has set in. Pleasant!" John pointed to the full moon, which just then became visible above the trees. "Ay, ay, I see, John: but what's the use of that? She always waits till your car-riage is upset, then pokes her lantern in your face to show you the mischief—makes a point of it in the country—never knew her act otherwise."

John, in the meanwhile, who had been surveying the position of the carriage with a view to its extrication, made a sign to the coachman to assist him in endea-vouring. to raise it, but, finding all his efforts ineffectual, he gave up the attempt, wiped his forehead, and walked off, simply saying,—"Get some one to help us."

"What! and leave me here to kick my heels in the mud with this deaf old had-dock of a coachman?" exclaimed Brown. "If I knew anybody in the three kingdoms who would be idiot enough to engage him, I would send him about his business tomorrow morning." So saying, he trudged briskly after John, whom he presently overtook, when they walked on in silence two or three hundred yards, until a turn-ing of the road disclosed to them a large old-fashioned house, standing close to the foot-path along which they were proceeding.

"Quite a respectable-looking residence," said Brown, well pleased with the dis-covery; and though the lower shutters are closed, the inhabitants can't be gone to bed. "What had we better do?"—John returned a practical answer by raising the heavy knocker, and giving three loud raps, which elicited no other response than their own dreary echoes sounding long and hollowly through the building, and then dying away into deep silence. Brown repeated his previous question, to which his companion replied by repeating the three blows more heavily than before. Scarcely had the knocker fallen for the third time when a piercing shriek resounded through the whole interior of the building; the glass of a window immediately above their heads was shivered with a loud smash; two fair and beautifully formed naked arms, from whose lacerated flesh the blood streamed down upon them, were protruded through it, waving with a ghastly horror in the moonlight; and, after another heart-rending scream, a female voice cried out, "Help, help! Oh, save him, save him!" [The ingenious author of 'Traits of Travel' (see vol. i. page 155 of that, work) must excuse this resumption of an incident originally communicated to him by the present writer, on the authority of one who actually witnessed its occurrence.]

"Gracious God!" ejaculated Brown, shuddering, as he started aside to avoid the blood, though the arms were suddenly withdrawn: "what is the meaning of this? They are perpetrating some horrid deed of villany within these walls, and we must try and scare the ruffians from their purpose. What, ho! hilloa! within there! open the door!" As he thus shouted out, raising his powerful voice to its loudest pitch, John renewed his knockings with an increased and incessant energy, but without effect; the mingled din died away as before in sepulchral echoes; a deep silence succeeded; and though they listened with breathless anxiety, they could not catch the sound of a footfall, nor any evidence of persons moving about, however stealthily, in the interior of the building.

Both were unarmed; and the sight and sounds we have described, proceeding from a lone house, might well have unnerved the stoutest heart; but John was absolutely insensible to fear, and, though Brown, as we have already intimated, was shy of unnecessary peril, he was not only a resolute man, but, where he suspected the perpetration of any cruelty or outrage, his indignation, and his eager desire to interfere and prevent it, made him a reckless one. Trotman's quick eye having detected a dilapidation in the wall that flanked the premises, he clambered over it, followed by his master, when they found themselves in a neglected garden, overgrown with rank vegetation. The shutter of one of the side windows was unfastened, the sash was up, and by the moonlight streaming through an open door opposite they could perceive that the room was large, old-fashioned, and unfurnished.

Seeming to think that he might claim precedence in this adventure without any disrespect to his master, John got in without noise, Brown did the same, they crossed the chamber and walked to the foot of a broad antique staircase, surmounted by a skylight. Both were silent, and both trod gently, as if they felt the prudence of stealing cautiously forward, where they might possibly be assailed by numerous desperadoes; but the creaking of the crazy stairs, reverberating in the hollow space, prated ominously of their whereabout, and accelerated the pulsation of Brown's heart, even while it urged him onward with a sterner resolution. On reaching the landing-place, John pointed to a door that stood ajar, with a significant look, which said, "*That* must be the chamber;" and at this instant they heard a low moaning sound from within, followed by the words—"It is *his* blood! it is *his* blood!" muttered in a shuddering sort of whisper, which occasioned Brown to grasp his cane with a convulsive energy. John pushed open the door, and they entered a spacious unfurnished room, at the further extremity of which, beside the broken window, and in the full glare of the moonlight, they beheld a female figure seated on the floor, repeating the words they had just heard, and moaning piteously as she gazed at her own bleeding arms,

"Poor dear creature!" exclaimed Brown, hastening up to her: "Heaven help us all! what a pitiful sight is this! Who are you? what are you? how came you in this unfurnished house?—You cried out Save *him:* to whom did you allude? Is any one with you? Were you seeking to escape, or have you cut yourself thus shockingly by accident?" Of these and other interrogatories put to her in rapid succession, she took no other notice than by reiterating the words, "It is *his* blood," followed by incoherent mutterings, and a wild vacant look, which manifestly declared her to be of unsound mind. "*Whose* blood?" demanded Brown. She glanced her eyes searchingly round the room, and only replied by a mournful shake of the head. John, in the mean while, without the loss of a single instant, hastily untied his neckcloth, tore it into strips, carefully examined her arms, and, having ascertained that they contained no portion of the broken glass, he bound up her wounds, which proved to be much less extensive than the effusion of blood had at first led them to fear. Having successfully accomplished this object, he whispered in his master's ear the word "mad," at the same time pointing to the full moon.

"Ay, ay; I see, I see," was the low-voiced reply. "Frightened perhaps by our knockings and shoutings, and under the influence of the full moon, the poor creature must have dashed her arms through the window, without knowing what she was about." John gave a nod, adding the words, "A lady," affirmatively.

"Evidently;" said his master, "and fair, and young, and delicate, and pretty too. Poor thing! poor thing! Whence on earth can she have come, and how can she have found her way to this empty and unfurnished house?"

"Married! again whispered his companion, pointing to a wedding-ring upon her finger.

"Adzooks! and so she is, I do protest. Ah! that's the secret, no doubt, of all her misfortunes. Same thing everywhere—go where you will—marriage at the bottom of all the mischief and misery. What fools people are! Well, thank God! *I* was never such an ass:—ha! ha!" He raised his cane, and was about to give the customary thumps, when, suddenly recollecting that it might startle or annoy the sufferer, he lowered it softly to the ground, for, spite of all his occasional roughness and petulance, Adam Brown had a gentle and a tender heart. "Why, John," he continued, "you are quite a surgeon; you have managed capitally: but what, in Heaven's name, are we to do with the poor lady?"

"Get coach-horse—ride for assistance," replied John, disappearing from the room almost as soon as the words were out of his mouth, and leaving his master in no small tribulation of mind. "Here's a pretty situation for a fellow to be placed in!" was his lugubrious exclamation, as he walked rapidly up and down the room from nervous excitement. "This is the infernal peace and happiness and security of a country life! Carriage upset in a ditch, coachman gone one way, footman another, and here am I, boxed up at night with a madwoman, in a lone unfurnished house. Shouldn't wonder if she were to bite me—both mad then—perhaps fight one another, like the two cats in the garret, until nothing left of either but a little bit of flue. Suppose the police were to find me here. Might be accused of having wounded her—taken up for a murderer if she dies. Swear away my life—shouldn't be surprised, not in the least: such things common where all is rural, innocence and simplicity! It would be only winding up the luck of the day."

These gloomy forebodings were soon dispelled; for when Trotman, running at full speed, reached the scene of the accident, he found that the coachman, with the assistance of some passing waggoners, had raised the carriage and drawn it from the ditch, undamaged, except by a few scratches, so that it was driven up to the door of the lone house, just as the grumbling merchant, following out the consequences of his soliloquy, imagined himself to be listening to his own last dying speech and confession. Delighted at being thus reprieved, as it were, at the foot of the gallows, he rubbed his hands gleefully, and told John that he had determined to take the poor lunatic lady to the Manor-House, and to keep her there until he could discover and restore her to her friends,—an announcement which was received with a nod of approbation.

"Hallo! what can be the meaning of this?" cried Brown, as he gently raised her from the floor in his arms: "her clothes are wringing wet, and yet we have not had a drop of rain."

"The Severn I" ejaculated John significantly, pointing at the same time to some fragments of river-weeds still adhering to her dress.

"Hey? how? Do you think, then, that the unhappy lady may have fallen into the river, or perhaps have thrown——"He paused, and John nodded, as he placed one of her wounded arms most carefully upon his own: his master did the same on the other side: and the object of their joint solicitude, who was now silent and perfectly passive, suffered herself to be led down-stairs, to be helped out of the window and over the wall, by which she had doubtless gained admittance into the house, and finally to be placed in the carriage. Brown seated himself beside her, Trotman mounted behind, the coachman drove off, and they reached the Manor-House without further accident, though not until a late hour.

CHAPTER II.

TRIALS and burthens are not to be measured by their actual weight, but by the powers and habits of those who are to endure them; and, thus tested, few will wonder that Allan Latimer's annoyances and disappointments, young and inexperienced as he was, should have plunged him into a state of great mental distress. Not only had his fond illusion with reference to Ellen been suddenly and painfully dispelled, but his feelings in every direction had been sorely wrung. To part thus suddenly, and for a period of which he saw not the termination, from the mother to whom he was so devotedly attached, and whom he had never hitherto quitted; from the brother whom he loved so dearly; from Adam Brown, whose friendship he had so many motives for cultivating, and whose disapproval of his flight had been so energetically expressed; from Woodcote, in which he had passed so many happy years; and to go forth upon the wide world, friendless and alone, without even any definite plan as to whither he should turn, or how he should employ himself—the violent severing of all these ties was like tearing his heart up by the roots. There was hope, indeed, at the bottom of the Pandora's box now opening before him, for he trusted that his voluntary exile might tend to prosper the fortunes and the loves of Ellen and Walter; but this wish, sweet and gratifying as it was, did not prevent the tears from gathering in his eyes, as he sat on the top of the London coach, almost unconscious whither he was wending, and too deeply immersed in his own sad thoughts to pay the least attention to his fellow-passengers.

Sometimes, while perusing plays or novels of which the scene was laid in London, he had felt a wish to visit the mighty metropolis, to inspect its time-hallowed and story-fraught public buildings, to gaze upon its magnificence, to mingle with its countless population, to enjoy for a short time its unrivalled shows and gaieties: but now that he was on the point of realising all that he had desired, his glittering aspirations faded altogether from his mind, and his thoughts reverted with a regretful yearning to the loved home from which he was flying, and where the current of his life had hitherto flowed on with such unvaried serenity and peace. Everything now recalled to him that happy home, the villages that he passed being only noticed that they might reflect back to him some feature of Woodcote. Every cottage that resembled his mother's, every green, or brook, or clump of trees, that bore the smallest likeness to similar objects in the vicinity of his abode, served but to increase his sadness; even the odours that were wafted from the fields or gardens were unrefreshing to his imagination, for they reminded him of the many delightful walks he had taken with his mother, or Ellen, or Walter, through scented bean-fields or by May-flower hedges—walks rendered still sweeter by that dear companionship—walks which perchance might never be resumed!

From this mournful reverie he was not awakened until they had completed nearly half their journey, when his attention was aroused by the somewhat singular appearance of a man who mounted the coach while the horses were being changed, and sat down beside him. Wrapped up in a large loose cloak, which concealed the whole upper portion of his form, his eyes encased in green goggles, while his throat and mouth were enveloped in a black respirator, such as is worn by persons of weak lungs, it was not easy to form a notion either of his general cast of countenance or of his age; but so far as an opinion might be risked from the contour of his form and the visible portion of his face, an observer would have guessed him to be young, and by no means uncomely. Concluding him to be an invalid, Allan, somewhat ashamed of the churlish silence he had hitherto maintained towards his fellow-travellers, expressed a hope that he experienced no inconvenience from the cold wind then blowing in their faces, adding that, if he were subject to any pectoral complaint, it might have been more prudent to travel inside.

"I thank you," replied the stranger, with a courteous bow, in a gentle voice, "but I am more incommoded by the confined air inside a coach than by the free atmosphere without, however sharp it may be, and you see I am well guarded against its attacks."

"I believe," resumed Allan, "that Cheltenham, and its vicinity, which I have just left, are considered very favourable for persons affected by pulmonary ailments. A friend of mine, who used to suffer much from asthma, finds himself considerably better since he came to reside under the Cotswold Hills, at a place called Woodcote."

"Woodcote!" ejaculated the stranger.

"Yes, you may possibly have heard of him; his name is Adam Brown."

"Adam Brown!" echoed the man, reddening suddenly, and fidgeting in his seat.

"Yes; do you know him?"

"Not I: how should I know him? Who is he? what is he?—where is Woodcote? I never heard of it. Never heard of him." His auditor was struck by the agitated manner and husky tone in which this was spoken, so different from the placid bland-ness of his previous demeanour; but, attributing it to the irritability of an invalid, he endeavoured to continue the conversation by some commonplace remarks on the scenery. His companion, however, made no reply, and, as the stage again moved on, he closed his eyes, nodded his head, and fell or appeared to fall into a deep sleep, so that Allan relapsed into silence and melancholy thoughts for another ten or twelve miles, when the stage again stopped to change horses, drawing up under a sign suspended over the middle of the road.

It chanced that, at this moment, a workman, bestriding the cross pole whence it hung, was securing it by an additional nail, for it had received some damage, when the noise of his hammer, arousing the stranger from his slumber, occasioned him to look suddenly up and to fix his eyes upon the carpenter for nearly half a minute, during which brief interval he drew the lower part of his face out of the respirator. At this moment Allan observed that he had a deep scar on the left side of his cheek,—a circumstance which he would probably have forgotten as soon as he had noticed it had he not recollected that Chubbs had described the mysterious monk as having an exactly similar mark. Coupling this fact with his evident emotion at the mention of Woodcote, he could not help fixing his eyes upon him with an eager and a penetrating look, which was no sooner detected by his fellow-traveller than he replaced the respirator in evident confusion, and changed his position to the back of the roof, merely saying that he was afraid to face the cold wind any longer.

This movement rather tending to confirm Allan's suspicions, he felt strongly tempted to sound him by making some allusion to Chubbs and his cart, but in his present position it was not easy to hold a parley with him, and, had it been practicable, he began to doubt after a little consideration, whether it would be justifiable. Chubbs had not spoken very positively as to this supposed cicatrice; even if he were correct in describing it, other men might be similarly marked; and he felt that he had no right to cross-question a fellow-traveller thus casually encountered, still less to presume that he had been engaged in a night adventure of so mysterious, not to say so disreputable, a character. Besides, the person they had seen in a monastic dress was represented, both by Chubbs and Brown, as old and bald-headed, whereas the individual who had just left his side was apparently young, and wore a bushy head of hair. As he was evidently, however, anxious to conceal himself, Allan, in spite of these discrepancies, continued to associate him with the runaway monk, and determined to keep his eye upon him during the remainder of the journey, in the hope that something might occur before they reached London to confirm or rebut his suspicions. Great, therefore, was his mortification on finding, when they again stopped, that he had left the coach, having got down, as it appeared, at the foot of the last hill and struck immediately into a cross-road. The coachman stated, when questioned on the subject, that he had never seen the gentleman before; that he had no luggage whatever, not even a carpet-bag; and that he had paid his fare to London. It was evident, then, that he had intended to proceed thither—a design which he would appear to have abandoned on account of the accidental exposure of his chin to the scrutiny of his fellow-traveller. Such, at least, was Allan's conjecture, which, whether well founded or not, furnished him with abundant materials for surmise and suspicion, and thus helped to withdraw his thoughts from the consideration of his own grievances.

Other considerations, suggested by the novel character of the objects surrounding him, tended to divert his attention, for he was now approaching the mighty metropolis of which he had heard, and read, and thought so much, but which had hitherto presented itself to his imagination as the dim and mysterious phantasm of a province covered with houses, churches, and palaces, rather than as a reality which was ever to be subjected to his waking senses. As yet its position was only signified by a distant and dense mass of vapours, whence the all-surmounting dome of St. Paul's heaved itself up into the air with a graceful majesty, or the gilded cross of some lofty spire would emerge for a moment in the shifting lights of a windy evening, again to be veiled in smoke-clouds, thus stimulating only to disappoint his curiosity.

Other and nearer changes attracted his notice as they proceeded. Handsomely appointed carriages of every description, bearing back the rich citizens to their country houses, passed them in quick succession; while the detached villas on either side the road, attesting in every detail the wealth of their occupants, exhibited an air of pretension and a class character of their own. Projecting porticoes, plaster pilasters, and ornamental entablatures of stucco, crowning the narrow wings, affected some claim to architectural design; the plate-glass windows, planted drive, flaunting flower-garden, and well-fenced paddock, wherein pastured two or three Alderney cows, or the eldest son's best hackney, dignified with the name of a hunter, showed that the citizen who could afford to live eight or ten miles out of town assumed in some little degree the character of a country gentleman.

As the travellers drew nearer to London, these villas were planted closer to each other, in narrower slips of ground, until at length they could only maintain their independence and isolation from their neighbours by a side doorway and a hall of a few feet diameter. This distinctive dignity shortly disappeared; the squeezed compact tenements assumed the form of streets, though a slip of front garden, planted with dingy poplars and sickly flowers, struggled by a few faint remnants of expiring rurality to preserve the neighbourhood from absolute Londonism. Again, as they whirled along, another change became manifest in the style of the suburban buildings. Smaller, meaner, dirtier, and still more densely wedged, the houses were brought close up to the foot-pavement for the convenience of the shops, and the narrow slip of garden, transferred to the back of the building, being used for drying linen, or for the purposes of trade, though even here a little patch of sooty green, or a few flowerpots, showed an unwillingness to allow the lingering smiles of nature to be altogether obliterated.

While noticing these successive mutations, Allan was struck by the busy throngs of people, the endless varieties of vehicles passing and re-passing, the ceaseless noises of wheels, and the clamour of the various cries—a grating dissonance which increased to a stunning bewilderment when the stage rattled over the paved stones, amid the whole clattering turmoil, and bustle, and hubbub of multitudinous London. A stoppage of some continuance upon Westminster Bridge, where the carriages were blocked up in an immovable mass, while the stream of passengers on either side flowed on without interruption, actually startled him by its strange silence, enabling him at the same time to survey the novel scene around him with a more leisurely and collected observation. A few yards in advance of the stage-coach stood a funeral procession, with its sable plumes, returning from a burial in the country;—from the deck of a steam-vessel, as it churned its foaming way through the waves beneath, sprang suddenly up the sound of jocund music, to the accompaniment of which a crew of male and female revellers were dancing merrily on the deck;—at a little distance were seen two boats dragging for the body of a female who had committed suicide by throwing herself from the bridge a few hours before; while both upon the land and water the mingled struggle of business and pleasure, of life and death, was plied with an eagerness that seemed to blind each participator to every fate and every object but his own.

At this moment a rather appalling thought flitted athwart the mind of Allan.

What if the bridge, unable to support the accumulated masses above, were to be precipitated upon the boats below! Such an idea, in all probability, had not occurred to a single other individual of the whole crowd. Use and daily transit had driven away all thought of danger: besides, when an accommodation of any sort has long continued, we think that it has no longer any right, scarcely indeed any power, to cease. But this was the first time that Allan had crossed so great a bridge, or seen so vast an assemblage.

On his left were the Houses of Parliament, with all their historical associations, and the venerable Abbey, beneath whose pavement reposed the silent dust which had composed the intellect and the vigour, the poetry, the science, the wisdom, and the valour of England, since first she had spread her arts and arms over the world, and had asserted her "proud pre-eminence of teaching the nations how to live." Turning his eyes in an opposite direction, he swept over the whole western expanse of the city, now glooming in the dim and congregated vapours of evening, and presenting few distinguishable objects but spires and domes, and an interminable succession of chimneys, each throwing up the smoky veil which was shortly to fall upon its head and hide it for the night.

"And each of those chimneys," thought Allan, for the houses were no longer visible, "communicates with family firesides, with gilded saloons or cobwebed hovels, with parties assembled for weal or woe, but at all events for the enjoyment of social fellowship; and in all this outstretched mass of buildings, in all this mighty metropolis with its myriad of inhabitants, I am without a single friend,—I am alone. In the solitude of the country there is nothing oppressive, nothing withering! for if we are withdrawn from man, we are brought into nearer and sweeter communion with nature; but to be exiled from her, and all her soul-cheering charms and influences, to stand alone in the desert of a crowded city, without a single sympathising bosom—to be *in* the world and not *of* it—this, this is indeed solitude; it is more than isolation, it is the living death of the heart."

So completely was he saddened and crushed by this feeling, that the increasing crowds as he advanced only deepened the sense of his loneliness, and he closed his eyes in order to shut out the sight of fellow-creatures with whom he had no fellowship, until the coach arrived at the Regent Circus, when he stepped down upon the London pavement with a prostration of spirit such as he had never before experienced. Mechanically following the waiter into the coffee-room, he stood in the midst of it for two or three minutes, gazing vacantly at the new scene around him, and hardly yet reconciled to the startling fact that he, a stranger, forlorn, helpless, and alone, should actually be deposited in the centre of that huge arena wherein a million and a half of human beings were incessantly engaged in the great struggle for subsistence, for distinction, or advancement. Unexcited by ambitious hopes, and unsolicitous for wealth or fame, what business had he, an humble and unaspiring man of the fields, in this fierce and whirring vortex, this metropolitan Maelstrom?

A waiter dispersed his reverie, and brought him back to the business which must be plied alike in town or country, by putting a bill of fare in his hands, and asking what he would be pleased to have for dinner. "Whatever is ready," was the reply,—an answer which summoned him in two or three minutes to a small table and a joint, whose aspect, however inviting, could not tempt him to eat; for where the head and the heart are full of busy thoughts and sad feelings, the pleading even of an empty stomach will not always be regarded. To Allan, who had never been in a coffee-room before, there was something singularly unsocial and selfish in the eager haste with which his neighbours, each at his own little table, gobbled up his allotted portion, without taking notice of anybody or anything but the viands before him. Though he could not imitate their voracity in this respect, he was so far influenced by the example of his immediate neighbours as to call for a tumbler of warm negus and some biscuits, which he had just concluded when the waiter brought him a newspaper, concluding that its perusal would induce him to order a fresh supply of the beverage. His eye fell listlessly upon the columns, but his thoughts were at Woodcote with his mother, with Ellen, with Walter; with all that he loved upon earth, and all now far, far away from him. As he evinced no disposition to order a replenishment of the tumbler, the waiter informed him that a gentleman would be glad of the paper as soon as it was out of hand,—an application which occasioned an immediate surrender of the broad sheet, and recalled his wandering thoughts.

He had intimated his intention of sleeping at the hotel, and, as he found the time beginning to hang heavy upon his hands, he resolved to gratify his curiosity by taking a short stroll in the immediate vicinity. Having arrived just at the hour of dusk, ere the shops were fully lighted, he was dazzled and amazed, when, upon turning into the Quadrant, he found himself surrounded by a blaze of splendour from the gas-illumined windows and lamps, eclipsing even the rays of the full moon, which were thrown slantingly through the inter-columnar spaces, only to fade before the glare of artificial light.

The beauty, the magnificence, the singularity of that double colonnade; the apparently interminable extent imparted to it by its winding course; the brightness of meridian day, when he had expected to step forth into the gloomy night; the variety and brilliance of the shops; the crowds of jostling pedestrians; the throng of whirling carriages in the serpentine street, seemed to his astonished senses an enchantment, a dream, that had conjured up some gorgeous scene out of the 'Arabian Nights,' or rather some vision of architectural grandeur, from the classic soil of Athens or Rome. Lost in ever-increasing admiration, he paced the Quadrant, on both sides, for upwards of an hour, when he returned to his hotel, and shortly retired to rest, anticipating some fantastic dream of the wonders he had seen; but he had scarcely laid his head upon the pillow when all vanished, and his brooding thoughts recurred—not without a feeling of self-reproach at their temporary alienation—to Woodcote, to his mother, to Ellen, to Walter.

Though his impetuous feelings had hurried him thus suddenly away from home, he had not been so entirely absorbed by them as not to have formed some plan, however vague and shadowy, as to his destination and employment in London. Determined not to withdraw one shilling from the narrow income of his family, already barely sufficient for his mother's comfort, he resolved to apply to a distant relation of the name of Lum, a house-agent and auctioneer, residing in Bloomsbury, and to solicit his aid in procuring for him some employment which might suffice to maintain him, until circumstances should allow his return to Woodcote. With this person the Latimers had held no communication for several years, but he Was remembered among them as a kind hearted thriving man of business, with a good many connections in the city, so that Allan deemed him the most likely person to promote his present views, at all events by his advice, if he could not immediately obtain for him a situation. What this might be, provided only that it were honourable, he cared not, for he had no false pride that he would suffer to interfere with the honest pride of independence.

Having studied a map of London until he had made himself master, as he thought, of the direct route to Bloomsbury, he sallied forth at an early hour of the following morning, again turning into the Quadrant, and again involuntarily stopping to admire its singular beauty, as well as the motley character of the people passing and repassing, who were already numerous. Spruce dapper clerks hurrying to the public offices, substantial shopkeepers walking from their westward or suburban residences, tradeswomen with their baskets and bundles, early Jews, and hawkers, all with eager business-like faces, afforded a strange contrast to a set of loungers, lodgers in the Quadrant or its immediate vicinity, dark, untoiletted, moustached, and bewhiskered men, mostly belonging to the Opera, the theatre, or gaming-houses, who sauntered out in slippers to smoke a cigar and while away half an hour before breakfast, or to gaze listlessly at the uninterrupted succession of omnibuses and other vehicles which were conveying a whole mercantile and trading population into the eastern quarters of the metropolis.

While thus occupied, Allan heard a sharp high-pitched voice ejaculate, *"Vinti mille diavoli!* three-fourths, three-fourths! Cospetto! what a Jew!"—The oath and the peculiar voice were familiar to his ear; he looked round, and beheld a little old man in rather shabby black, with an aquiline nose and a large dark eager eye, carrying his left arm in a sling, while the other leaned upon an umbrella as he paused for a moment in apparent communion with his own impatient thoughts. "Signor Crevetti," exclaimed Allan, "I am delighted to see you. Who would have thought that we should thus meet in London? Instantly dropping his right hand over the gold seals of his watch with an assumed air of nonchalance, but with an evident intention to protect those appendages, the Italian peered up in the face of his interrogator, wearing a look of searching though silent suspicion.

"No wonder you have forgotten me," said Allan; "it is some time since we met, and yet I saw you often enough when I went over to Cheltenham to take lessons of you on the violoncello. You then used to say that Allan Latimer was the most promising of all your pupils."

"Allan Latimer? *Maraviglioso!* So it is! Ah, you played beautiful, beautiful." And so saying, he tucked the umbrella under his arm, and shook his pupil's hand with a real cordiality which he would not have lavished on any but a good performer on his favourite instrument. Taking Allan's arm, and leading him along the Colonnade, the old Italian questioned him as to the cause of his visiting London, and soon obtained from his companion, who was naturally frank and unreserved, the full particulars of his little history, at the conclusion of which he again stopped, and inquired, with an anxious look, whether he had continued his practice of the violoncello.

"Continued!" exclaimed Allan; "I have done little else: it has become a passion with me, and I have been sometimes blamed for throwing away so much time upon it."

"Throw away, throw away!" cried the Italian with an indignant gesture. "What do the fools suppose time was made for? And you play better—*molto meglio*—than when we parted?"

"I think you will say so."

"*Bene, bene!* and you will let me hear you. Stay—stay—*aspettate un poco.* Can you come now to my lodgings?—just by—quite *vicino*".—Allan having given a willing assent, they turned into Swallow-street, were admitted by a dirty-looking maid-servant into a narrow door beside a handsome shop, and climbed up three pair of stairs, when the Italian took a key from his pocket, and inducted his companion into a well-furnished apartment of good dimensions, though the atmosphere, suffused with the mingled odours of coffee and snuff, smelt close and unwholesome. "I never open my window," said Crevetti, who seemed to be aware of this little peculiarity, "because the fog and the damp air he spoil the string—in one *cinque,* one five minute, down he go, one half- note below concert pitch." This must have been an object worth consideration, there being two violoncellos in the room, besides a huge bass in the corner, and several violins dispersed about. *"Via! scolajo mio,"* cried the master—"There is my own violoncello, the best in all England,—all but two and three others: he is tuned this morning; what shall you play?" Allan's eye fell upon some manuscript music on a stand: it was the tender, the mournful, the pathetic passage from the 'Sonnambula,' the *Tutto e sciolto*—the very piece which he had lately been practising with the greatest assiduity, because it had appealed the most touchingly to his feelings. "Anything you like," replied Allan, with the excusable vanity of wishing to surprise his old master.

"*Bene, bene!* he is beautiful," replied Crevetti, pointing to the score, seating himself where he could best observe the handling of the instrument, and taking a previous pinch of snuff that he might not interrupt the performance. After repeated and most energetic cries of *"Bravo! bravissimo!"* accompanied by vehement gesticulation and amazed upliftings of the shaggy grey eyebrows, Crevetti, when his pupil had concluded, started from his seat, threw his right arm around him, hugged him, kissed his cheek, and then almost danced around him, ejaculating, amid mingled bursts of English and Italian, that he actually wanted words to express his amazement,—an averment which was perhaps meant as an excuse for his almost convulsive demonstrations of delight. "My dear Sir," he at length exclaimed in a tone of profound respect, for he no longer looked upon him in the familiar light of a pupil—"my dear Sir, I am *tutto stupefatto:* you beat your old master all to a nothing—all the world beat him now. *Ecco!* look here:" and he drew his bandaged hand from its sling. "One two days ago, the lid of a heavy piano fall on him, a hook tear him,—there come a—how you call him?—a *postema,*—an imposthume;—and here I am, lame of all my fingers for a *quindici,* for a fortnight,—perhaps for as much more."

"This is unfortunate," said Allan, "for of course it prevents you playing."

"*Totalmente.* I cannot give my lessons; I cannot play at the Opera,—benché, *I am one of the band.* Ben bene, *when I met you, I had just seen Carlini: ah! he is a* furbo, *quite a* misero, *that old fellow. I showed him my hand, and said, 'What shall I pay you to give my lessons till I am well of this* maledetto affare?*' And he told me, 'Three-fourths of what you charge.'* Vinti mille diavoli! and the old Jew call himself my friend!"

"Not a very friendly offer, I must confess."

"*Ben bene,* this is what I say to you. *Ecco,* my dear Sir! You want to get a little money for a short time. You shall give my lessons for me. *Si, si!* you must not shake your head,—you are quite able. You shall give my lessons, and I will pay you one-half—*mezzo,*—you understand: how say you?"—Looking upon a musical performer or teacher of any sort as one of the most elevated characters of existence, it did not for a moment occur to Crevetti that his young friend, although he had hitherto enjoyed a state of humble independence, would consider his proposition in any way derogatory. Nor did it so present itself to Allan, who, being free from any conventional prejudices of that nature, and determined not to encroach upon the narrow income of his family, accepted the offer, only stipulating that it should be immediately cancelled in case he should prove incompetent to the discharge of its duties. At Crevetti's suggestion, and for the convenience of both parties, he engaged a comfortable bed-room in the same house, agreeing to take his meals, as often as it might suit him, with the Italian, who generally dined at a French *restaurateur's* in the immediate neighbourhood, when he did not make a sausage and a couple of French rolls at home a substitute for that repast. His portmanteau was accordingly transferred to Swallow-street, and Allan Latimer found himself, although he could hardly credit the reality of so sudden a change, an inhabitant of London.

CHAPTER III.

SCARCELY had he been installed in his new apartment when Crevetti, who had disappeared for half an hour, bustled back into the room, forcing half a pinch of snuff up his hook nose, and distributing the remainder over the floor, while he shrilly ejaculated—"*Via!* my young friend—for I call you now my scholar no more—*fortunatamente,* I found her just come down, just going to breakfast; and she say to me—*Cielo!* how she is always *amabile!*—let your friend come at one o'clock, *ad un' ora,* and he shall accompany me."

"Of whom are you talking?" demanded Allan.

"*Come?* did I not tell you? Of Signora Guardia. You know her, of course?"

"No, indeed; I never heard of the lady."

"*Epossibile?* is he possible?" ejaculated the Italian, while his eyebrows, uplifted in wonder, drove a succession of wrinkles up his brown forehead, like the wave-worn ripples upon the sands of the sea-shore. "Not heard of the *cantatrice,* the famous contralto singer? *bellissima voce!—Ebbene,* I was to accompany her on the violoncello at a grand concert, where the Guardia is to sing Donizetti's aria,—oh! he is beautiful!—out of the 'Torquato Tasso,'—*Io l'udia nei suoi bet carmi* You recollect him?—*Si, si,* you play him to me at Cheltenham."

"I know it well; I have lately been practising the accompaniment."

"*Per buona ventura,*—good, good! *Ecco,* you shall rehearse him this morning with the Guardia; and if she is content with your play, you shall accompany her at the concert: *che dite?* Ah, she will like you, *molto, molto!*"

"If you think I am equal to it."

"Bah! you shall have no fear: set you to work in ***questo punto,***—now, directly. There is the score; ***via!*** I will sit here and listen to you. Wait you till I take my snuff."—The passage, as Allan had stated, being quite familiar to him, the bravos and delight of his auditors were not less exuberant and noisy than on his previous performance; but as some trifling amendments were suggested, it was played a second and a third time, until the critic, who was so devoted to music that he could hear the same piece ten times repeated, provided the execution were of a high order, at length pronounced it to be faultless.

"Have you a servant here who can carry the violoncello round to the Signora's?" demanded Allan, as the time drew near for their appointment.

"Si, si," replied the Italian—"the best servant in the world—***io medesimo.*** How says your proverb? He is a bad horse that will not carry his own—how you call it? ***Bene, he*** is my provender, and I shall carry him like a good horse. ***Cospetto!*** I should be an ass to pay just for to carry him round the corner." With these words he encased his favourite violoncello in a green bag, performing that operation as carefully as if it had been a delicate child; and had it indeed been his own flesh and blood, he could scarcely have appeared to love it more tenderly. Allan made some joking allusion of this nature, when the old man kissed the instrument with great emotion, exclaiming—"***Ebbene!*** he is my child, my only child; and when he keeps in good tune and I am well content of my play, I always kiss him and tell him 'You have been a good boy.' He was once the ***favorito*** of Dragonetti, but he never love him as I do." So saying, he placed his darling under his arm, and bore his burden carefully along the Quadrant, until they reached the door of the Signora's residence, which was opened by an old grey-headed and grey-suited Italian, who began instantly chatting with Crevetti in his own language. No sooner however had his eye fallen upon Allan than he started with an expression of some surprise, and, after again peering at his features, slowly but emphatically muttered a few words to himself, whereof the import was not to be distinguished.

The drawing-room into which the visitants were ushered was of handsome dimensions and appearance, looking out upon the top of the colonnade, which, instead of being pierced with a sky-light, as in most , of the adjoining houses, presented the level surface of a little garden, ornamented with evergreens, shrubs, and exotic flowers. In the apartment, which at the moment of their arrival was unoc-cupied, might be observed the usual profusion of furniture and trinketry, scattered about with the air of disorderly *nonchalance* prescribed by fashion; but the whole was fresh and neatly kept. Music scores of various operas were heaped confusedly on the grand piano; a superb Persian robe, intended to be worn at the next opera performance, reposed upon the back of a handsome *fauteuil;* musical boxes, and Italian as well as English books, littered the tables; a beautiful though small figure of Psyche stood on a console; and the room was suffused with the odour of a tuberose planted in a handsome china vase, by the side of which hung a canary-bird in a gilt cage. While Allan made these observations, his companion had been gingerly with-drawing the violoncello from its case, and arranging the music-stand,—operations which he had just concluded when a side-door opened, and the Signora hurried in, apologising to Crevetti, with a singularly gracious expression and melodious voice, for having kept him waiting.

Isola Guardia, for such was the name of the fair vocalist, appeared to be about twenty years of age, though she possessed so much mutability both of form and fea-ture, that in her varying moods she might be supposed some years older or younger. Her lustrous hair, of the raven's purplish black, braided close to her face, displayed to advantage the fine and classical shape of her head,—a beauty seldom appreciated as it ought to be. Her large bright hazel eyes, fringed with long lashes, surmounted by finely arched distinctly-marked brows, and an expansive forehead, imparted to the upper portion of her face a character of the finest Italian order, lofty, command-ing, and beautifully statuesque; while the lower half participated somewhat of the Spanish type, the lips being rich and full, and the cheeks dimpled, as was also the round and rather short chin; thus presenting an appearance that might have been deemed voluptuous, had not her countenance been chastened by an expression of perfect though gracious modesty. No fixed colour was visible in her dark clear complexion, but its place was well supplied by the changeful hues, the thousand blushing apparitions, which chased each other over her features, according to the varying emotions of her mind. From the perfect symmetry of her form, her stature, which was rather above than below the middle height, appeared less than it really was; but even with reference to her figure, so different were the aspects she could make it assume, that a spectator might have found it difficult to pronounce whether the majestic dignity of the Roman girl, or the supple gracefulness of the Andalusian, were most conspicuous in her carriage and *tournure.*

In her cordial welcome of Crevetti, she had not immediately perceived Allan; but no sooner had her looks rested upon him than she started as the servant had done, stopped suddenly in her approach, and, with wide-opened eyes, elevated brows, and a mouth just sufficiently unclosed to reveal her pearly teeth, remained gazing for an instant in evident amazement, after which she ejaculated in perfect English—"Good Heavens! never, no never did I see such a likeness. I beg your pardon," she continued, gracefully curtsying and pointing to a chair, for Allan remained standing—"but you bear so striking a resemblance to a near and dear relation whom I have left in Italy, that I could almost have imagined it to be himself. Ohimè—there is no such happiness. Yes, you are the very image of Camillo."

"Is it a brother whom I have the good fortune so closely to resemble?" asked Allan.

"Excuse my rudeness in again gazing at you," resumed Isola—"No, I shall never be able to call you anything but Camillo."

"I shall be only too proud to answer to that name, and to deem myself indeed your brother, if I may be so far honoured."

"Camillo! your sister holds you to that bargain," said the beautiful Italian, at the same time extending her hand with such a winning and affectionate, yet modest and blushing cordiality, that Allan could not refrain from pressing it respectfully to his lips.

"I dare say you think me very forward, considering this is our first interview," faltered Isola, withdrawing her hand in some little confusion; "but a brother and sister, you know—and besides, Crevetti will tell you that, though I am an odd girl, there is no harm in me."

"*Si, si, si,*" cried the old Italian, in the intervals of as many pinches of snuff; "una fanciulla—without a fault. Every way you are as good as you sing charming: how can you then be more good? *Via!* let us begin. All is ready,—he is in good tune."

"Stay, stay!" exclaimed Isola, ringing the bell. "I must first ask Antonio whether the likeness strikes him as forcibly as it does me. It will gratify the dear old man." With the kindness which in Italy makes the servant one of the family, and which, by securing his respectful attachment, proves that familiarity does not always breed contempt, she fell into chat with Antonio, asking him in Italian whether her new visitant reminded him of any friend at Naples, in answer to which he immediately pronounced the word Camillo, and declared that he had no sooner opened the door than he had been struck by the likeness.

"Ah! I was sure of it—I was sure of it. Dear, dear Camillo!" exclaimed Isola, with a tender sigh: and then, dismissing Antonio, she apologised to Allan with the utmost suavity and grace for having detained him so long, and declared that she was ready to begin.

"Grazie a Dio!" cried Crevetti. "What signify brother and sister and likeness, and all that, when you might have something from the 'Torquato Tasso' of Donizetti?—so beautiful he is!"

Although this was only a rehearsal in her own apartment, Isola, not unwilling perhaps to make a favourable impression upon her new acquaintance, or possibly because the associations he had called up had deeply interested her feelings, threw her whole soul into the passage where she proclaims her readiness to resign both crown and kingdom, could she be thus assured of her lover's truth. Standing up as she sang, and partially assuming the attitudes and expression appropriate to the character she represented, the queen-like dignity of her figure, which seemed to expand as she proceeded, the play of her most eloquent and beautiful features, the mellow richness of her contralto tones, presented a combination of charms which might have overpowered Allan, had not a great portion of his attention been necessarily confined to his own book and his own performance, Enough, however, had been seen and heard to raise. his admiration and delight to ecstacy; nor was this feeling diminished when the gifted songstress, addressing him as her brother Camillo, and protesting that she had never been better accompanied in her life, expressed her wish that he should supply the place of Signor Crevetti at the coming concert,—a proposition to which he gave an eager and delighted assent.

At Crevetti's request, he now played over again the *Tutto e sciolto* from the 'Sonnambula,' performing it with so much emotion and pathetic tenderness, under the inspiration of his own softened feelings and Isola's beaming eyes, that she exclaimed as he concluded, while her looks and tones attested that her words came from her heart—"Beautifully, exquisitely played indeed! Methought I could hear your instrument actually speak, or rather sigh, the words— *'il piu tristo dei mor-tali;'*—but, surely, surely, *you* can have no. reason to call yourself unhappy."

"Not to-day, not to-day at all events, whatever I may have thought yesterday," replied Allan.

"And he was my pupil!" exclaimed Crevetti, drawing himself up and rubbing his hands triumphantly.

"And he is your master," laughed Isola.

"Venti mille diavoli! Si—but for why? because I am *monco*—lame of my hand. *Ahi!* how he pain me!"

Although the beautiful Italian spoke with a foreign accent, which, however, only imparted a more pleasing piquancy to her dulcet tones, she possessed a perfect command of the language, for which she accounted to Allan, when he expressed his surprise at her fluency, by telling him that her mother had been an Englishwoman, married to an Italian singer at Naples, where both her parents died. The canary-bird, who had been silent during the playing and singing, now set up a loud and shrill piping, as if determined to drown the conversation since he could not take a share in it. "That is always his way," said Isola; "he will listen all day to vocal or instrumental music, but it seems as if he could not endure talking."

"*Si,* and a very sensible bird too: conversation is all throw away time," cried Crevetti, "*tutto perduto!* my violoncello he talk much better than me."

"Granted," smiled Isola: "but the bird forgets that there are others in the room, so I must check his volubility." With these words she threw a black veil over the cage, which immediately silenced the little warbler, when she continued, with an altered tone and look, "And yet, poor little fellow! I cannot help sympathising with him, for our fates are nearly similar. An exile from his native land, his cage, though gilded and adorned, is only a prison, in which he is compelled to sing for his subsistence. Exposed to all the severities of an ungenial climate—Oh! how unlike his own sunny land! he is not only doomed to struggle with the instinct of migration, but may perchance be pining for the mate from whom he has been severed. That, that is indeed a cruel trial."

Her voice softened as she spoke, her eyes assuming at the same time an expression of peculiar tenderness, which was presently succeeded by an indignant flash, as she resumed, "And then, when people are tired of the poor bird, or the poor *can-*

tatrice, they throw over their heads the dark veil of silence and oblivion. Our life is only a sound, our memory is only its faint echo."

"Basta!" cried Crevetti: "no more of this **dolente istoria.** I will not have you to be melancholic, though you are in England. I am never **tristo** while I can have my pinch of snuff and my violoncello. Ah, he is a darling!" Allan was about to make some reply to Isola's desponding observations, when the door opened, and Antonio, with a smile flickering over the grim mahogany of his features, like gold-leaf upon gingerbread, announced Mr. Tittup, a person usually designated in the purlieus of the minor theatres and the Opera House as little Tom Tittup.

Proud of his figure, which was in much better preservation than his face, his lower limbs were accurately outlined by tight elastic pantaloons, succeeded by silk stockings, not particularly clean, and a pair of dress shoes; while his upper man was screwed into a swallow-tailed coat, so pinched at the waist, that, but for the concealed belt, the buttons must have dragged their anchors. For reasons rendered evident by the chinchilla stubble left behind, his whiskers had been cut off. A flaxen wig, incongruously young, made his sharp dry features appear additionally old; nor was this tendency lessened when it was viewed from behind, where truant patches of straight grey hair, escaping at the nape of his neck, contrasted strangely with the hyacinthine juvenility of his purchased curls. Clear as it was, from these and other symptoms, that Tom was a **ci-devant jeune homme,** he was still young enough to discharge with efficiency the manifold duties of his calling,—that of a subordinate dancer, singer, and actor of all-work at one of the minor theatres. On the nights when his talents were not thus put in requisition, he was generally to be found at the Opera, if he could procure an order; failing in which, he usually indulged in a cigar and a tumbler of brandy and water at the Taglioni in Panton Street.

Jerking himself into the room on the tips of his toes, he advanced towards Isola, cut a very creditable **entrechat,** sank down upon one knee, and said, or rather sang in a sort of burlesque recitative,

"Dear Signora, **bella Cantatrice!** O listen to my prayer, I do beseech ye."

Lending herself to his fantastic humour, the person thus addressed threw herself into a theatrical attitude, and recitatived in reply, with a mock gravity that gave a rich zest of ridicule to her trifling words—

"I cannot listen to you thus—so sit up, And tell me your petition, Mister Tittup."

"O peerless songstress of the heavenly choir! O Signora, such as was never seen before-a!" apostrophised the actor; "ne'er will I rise up from my knee until you grant my humble plea. What says Pope, the bard of Twickenham; of the grotto, of the willow-tree? Saith he not that 'order is Heaven's first law'? And would you, beautifulissima,—have you the heart, O charmingissima, to prevent my enjoying the first law of Heaven?"

"In plain English," laughed Isola, "you want a gallery or a pit order for Saturday night. O most unreasonable Tittup! you promised not to apply to me again for a fortnight."

"Signora, you are truth itself; so much so, that you ought at this very moment to be lying at the bottom of a well. I did make you that promise,—the soft impeachment Tommy Tittup owns,—but I knew not then that *you* were to sing on Saturday; *you,* the muse of tuneful song, the Sappho of Leucadia's leap, the syren of the listening wave, the nightingalia of the warbling grove, whom if I hear not I shall die the death! Ah! those smiling eyes confirm my heart's best hope. You would not annihilate Tom Tittup."

"If you've no order for the pit, bestow Two for the gallery, and let me go."

"I have a great mind to give you none, as a punishment for your insincerity. My singing, indeed! Confess, O recreant knight, thou lover of the light fantastic toe—confess that you go to the Opera for the sole delight of seeing your friend Harriet Hogg—I beg her pardon, I mean Mademoiselle La Hogue—perform *pirouettes* in the ballet"

"O Signora, what a libel dire! Honour bright, as the stars shine by night! I go for the aria, the cavatina, the preghiera, the recitativo, and all the rest of that sort of thing-o. What! have you not heard that I am a vocalist and a composer, like yourself?"

"I have heard one of your *preghiere,*—that which prays for pit or gallery orders,—which you yourself have encored till I am weary of it."

"Then will I sing you a bran new one, that shall make your delighted ears stand on end, like quills upon the fretful porcupine. Talk of the *Fra nembi crudeli,* from the 'Brigand,'—of *Al mio pregar t' arrendi,* from 'Otello,'—of the still more touching one from 'Anna Bolena,'—what are they all compared to the pathetic solemnity of mine? List, list, oh list, to mine, addressed to the goddess of the light fantastic toe!—

"Grant, O Terpsichore, Goddess of kickery, Entrechats, pirouettes, capers, That when I shall play In next Friday's ballet, My *pas seul* may be puff'd in the papers."

These absurd words, sung to a ludicrous tune, with a still more ludicrous mimicry of operatic vehemence and gesticulation, occasioned Isola to burst into a peal of laughter, which, though silvery in sound, exhibited all the hearty and joyous abandonment of a child.

"Really, Tittup," she exclaimed, "this is excellent foolery,—it is irresistible. I can refuse you nothing. Dancing, poetry, and song, all at once! Truly you are the great Apollo of the minor theatres, and shall be crowned as you deserve." With these words, she snatched a pit ticket from the mantelshelf, hummed a light air, to the accompaniment of which she danced twice round the kneeling figure, with a grace and elegance that might well be termed the poetry of motion, while the radiant smiles chased each other over her face like sunbeams on the waves, and then, depositing the ticket upon his flaxen poll, and suddenly changing the expression of her features, she chanted in sonorous recitative,—

"For your light heart, light heels, light hair, light face, This tribute on your lighter head I place.

And thus concludes the farce, and Mr. Tittup may rise from his kneeling posture," she added in her natural voice, at the same time pointing to a chair. The actor of all-work arose in apparent obedience to the intimation, but, as he never lost an opportunity of displaying his agility, he first took his position behind the chair, placed his hands upon the back, vaulted over it into the seat, jumped thence to the ground, sat himself down, twiddled his thumbs rapidly round each other, and looked with a smirk of infinite self-satisfaction into the face of each of his companions, as much as to say, "There, what do think of that?"

"I should just like to know," said the performer of this feat, after a short interval, during which he seemed to be waiting for the applause of the spectators—"I should just like to know, merely for curiosity—but I *should* just like to know which of our bigwigs at any of our great meetings can take the chair in that style. Will the Lord Mayor attempt it in the Egyptian Hall, or any of the Court of Aldermen, or the Speaker of the House of Commons, or the Lord Chancellor in the Upper House, or

His Majesty (God bless him!) when he has to take the stone chair at the coronation? If they did, I should be particularly sorry to be the nose either of the Lord Mayor, or the Alderman, or the Speaker, or the Chancellor, or of His Majesty (God bless him!)—that's all *I* say, for I think there's very little doubt that they would fall flat upon it."

Isola now made some bantering allusion to his flirtation with Mademoiselle La Hogue, which he received with an affected confusion, as if he disclaimed all pretension to the exclusive regards of that lady, and then, having secured the great object of his visit, he started up, laid his hand upon his heart, flourished a bow of tender acknowledgment, followed by a demi-pirouette to Isola, kissed and waved both hands to Allan. and Crevetti, and danced and ***glissaded*** out of the room. Scarcely-a minute had elapsed from his disappearance when a slight scuffle was heard on the stairs, and an angry female voice, ejaculating, "Get along with you, you nasty old jackadandy!" which objurgatory words were found to proceed from the housemaid, who had accidentally met Tittup on the stairs, when he protested that he was under the unavoidable necessity of kissing her, because she had the true La Hogue eyebrow. Conquering, however, the unavoidable necessity, the culprit had taken to flight the moment he heard the opening of the drawing-room door; and Isola was probably right when she gave it as her opinion that he had merely ventured upon this little escapade to procure the reputation of being as gallant and as gay a Lothario among the housemaids as he was reputed to be, probably with equal reason, among the ballerinas of the Opera.

"I believe the poor fellow to be half-cracked," she added; "but as he is a kind-hearted creature, always ready to do a good office for any of his brother performers, and as I am really amused with his fustian and rhodomontade, I suffer him to plague me for free admissions."

"***Si, si,*** you are always kind, very kind, ***molto,***" cried Crevetti; "but why talk you of his fair hair? ***Cospetto!*** he is a wig, I know where he buy him. Why did you not quiz him, that fine curling wig?"

"Because I would not hurt poor Tittup's feelings,—and why should I? If you love your joke better than your friend, you will be very apt to lose your friend, which is no joke. I bantered him about La Hogue because I know he likes it. Every man of a certain age likes to be suspected of affaires du cœur; ***and I might per-***

haps bring a similar accusation against you, did I not know that you will never be cavaliere servente to any one but your lady love with the four strings,—your violoncello."

"Vero! vero!" cried the old man, throwing his arm affectionately round the instrument; "he is my darling, *gioja mia,* my innamorata."

"Ah! you are admiring my Psyche!" cried Isola to Allan, who had only withdrawn his eyes from herself, because he feared that his fixed and ardent gaze might appear rude. "Is it not beautiful? It is the work and the gift of my dear, dear Camillo." Electrified as it appeared by the bare mention of this name, she ran up to the figure, and repeatedly kissed it. "Do not take me for a Pygmalion in petticoats," she continued, while a slight blush swept across her face like a flash of rose-light: "I love the gift, because it reminds me of the giver."

"Is your brother then a statuary?" demanded Allan.

"Who, Camillo? Yes, a young one, but I hope to see him a distinguished artist when he is older. Wherever I have been since I left Italy, this image accompanies me."

"It is exquisitely imagined, as well as sculptured; and you could not well have selected a more appropriate companion in your travels, if it must be a statue, for I should imagine you, like Psyche, to be all soul."

"Only when I have this image in my thoughts—in my heart. You see Camillo has given her the wings of a butterfly. Metamorphosed from an earthworm to a tenant of the upper air, what a lucky symbol did that insect supply to the Greeks of the resurrection of the human body and the immortality of the soul! No wonder they sculptured it on their tombs."

"I know not a more beautiful fable, altogether, than that of Psyche."

"May we not rather call it an allegory? and perhaps the most ancient one in the world, for the Pagans seem to have borrowed it from higher and holier sources than any that their own mythology could supply. To me at least it has always appeared to shadow forth the disobedience and fall of the soul, and its redemption by Divine love."

"This little image may well be dear to you, since it suggests so many and such interesting associations."

"It may appear fanciful to say so, but I care little for any realities that do not stimulate the imagination. Will you think me very, very silly, if I declare myself passionately fond of a pantomime?"

"I never saw one, but I have always heard that they were only fit to amuse children."

"And I like them as a child,—nay, I can laugh till I cry at their mere foolery. And yet I see something in them that lifts them out of it, for I can fancy the first pantomime to have been a rude dramatising of the story of Cupid and Psyche. Harlequin is Mercury, whose sword or Caduceus can render him invisible, and transport him whither he will; Columbine is Psyche, or the soul, whom he wants to carry off to heaven; while the Pantaloon is Charon, who seeks perpetually to drag it down to the infernal regions. The Clown, with his mouth painted to resemble the ancient comic masks, is Momus, the buffoon of heaven. Did you ever read Dr. Clarke's Travels? He tells us that he has seen all these figures represented on an ancient vase, very much as they are now exhibited in our pantomimes."

"You have given me a new interest in this the most suggestive of all stories."

"I fear I must wish you good morning, for I have an engagement at the Opera House."

"It is understood, then, that I am to have the honour of accompanying you at the concert."

"Oh, certainly, certainly; but——"She paused; and an arch yet deprecating, smile made her look more winningly beautiful than ever as she continued, "Now you are going to think me very rude, and you will be very wrong; for one may be uncivil in speech, and yet polite in intention; or polite in speech, and very much the reverse in intention; and my freedom is of the former kind. You have just arrived from the country, I see." As her quick eye glanced over his habiliments, Allan caught her meaning and coloured.

"A young man, and yet blush! Nay then it is evident you have not been long in London. You will soon get over that weakness—perhaps by the time you have tried on your new clothes. Pray, pray, excuse my sauciness. With such a figure and deportment you can never look otherwise than like a gentleman, but nothing is so fatal to a young man upon his preferment in London as the slightest breath of ridicule, and above all the reputation of being a quiz. People will forgive you a gross deviation from morality much more easily than a slight one from fashion. Besides, if you don't do justice to yourself, how can you expect it from others?"

"I will lose no time—I am only just arrived—indeed I was not aware—"stammered Allan, abashed at the thought that his rusticity should be so obvious.

"Charming! charming!" exclaimed Isola; "it is really quite a study, as well as a treat, to see a young man—and such a young man!—standing confused and blushing in my presence, instead of exhibiting the brazen and insolent assurance to which I have been too much accustomed. **Will** you shake' hands with me, in token of forgiveness?"

"May I venture," asked Allan, as he held and gently pressed her small soft hand, "may I venture to call again when I shall be less unfashionably attired?"

"Believe me, Mr. Latimer—No, I will not call you by that name—Believe me when I say that I shall always be most happy to see—Camillo."

Words, however friendly or fervent, are nothing in themselves,—a *caput mortuum,* a body without a soul. They derive their life, their significancy, their power, from the tone and look with which they are accompanied. Isola's parting expressions were pronounced with such a frank and tender yet bashful earnestness, while her beaming eyes attested their sincerity, that Allan felt a thrill vibrate through his whole frame as he quitted what appeared to him a scene of enchantment, a fairy bower, a bewitching dream,—and found himself once more in the Quadrant, with old Crevetti by his side.

CHAPTER IV.

"NEVER, no never," he ejaculated, as he walked away, quite unconscious what direction he was taking, "have I seen so fascinating, so irresistible a creature! Why, Signor Crevetti, you never told me that she was so exceedingly beautiful."

"*Si, si,* I tell you always she had a beautiful voice; what signify her face? *Niente, niente,*—I never look at it when I hear her sing. My eyes are in my ears."

"It is not only the witchery of her singing, her face, her figure; but did you ever see anything so exquisitely graceful, and yet so perfectly ladylike, as her dancing?"

"*Si,* I tell you what was more graceful, *molto,*—her look, her tone, her expression, so all-soul-full, when she sang the words,

"Io l'udia nei suoi bei carmi. Trona e corona involami."

"That indeed was most touching; it seemed to come from her heart of hearts, and I am sure it went to mine. And then again, apart from all her professional talents and personal charms, what intelligence, what information, what cleverness!"

"Vero, vero! wonderful clever. Not a cavatina of Meyerbeer but what she will sing you at sight."

"But, young as she is, where did she contrive to pick up so much knowledge of books and things?"

"Oh, her mother have had her well educated when she was quite a *piccolina*—she loves to read books—she keeps her eyes open, and her ears *anche;* and so every day she picks up a something, per più, per meno."

"And her amiability seems equal to her other rare gifts. How playfully she lent herself to the humours of that crazy actor, and how kindly she spoke of him after he had gone!"

"Ah, she is kind in many ways—she plays every kind of music on the piano like an angel."

"And Whence does she come, this marvellous creature, this miracle of nature? Who is she? what is she? Do you know anything of her history?"

"What I know of him I can tell you in *poche parole.* Her mother, *dama Inglese,* was a singer at San Carlos,—you know him,—the great theatre at Naples. *Ebbene,*—her father, *si dice,* was a *bandito,* a captain of—how you call?—freebooters, from the mountains, who come to Naples to be cured of a bad wound, and made a vow to San Giacomo, if he got well, to—how you say it?—*menare una vita onesta.* Così, he got well; and as he have a great voice,—*basso superbo,*—he become a singer at San Carlos, he marry the beautiful Inglese, and they have a daughter born in the island of Ischia, perché they call her Isola; so you see she has fine voice of both sides of her parentage."

"And she is an orphan, is she not?"

"*Si.*"

"And that is all you know of her history."

"*Tutto.*"

Notwithstanding this assurance, Allan continued to ply his companion with questions on the same subject, until, suddenly recollecting her objections to his attire, he requested to be taken to some fashionable tailor without loss of time. Though always neatly dressed, he had hitherto been indifferent as to conformity with the last new mode; in the country, one slips unconsciously into this sort of carelessness; but, feeling now as if he were not producible, he determined neither to call upon the Lums nor any of Crevetti's pupils until he should have received a new, and in every respect a modish, equipment. A little addition to the price procured a speedy accomplishment of his wishes, and, within two days of his arrival in London, Allan, whose singularly handsome person and graceful carriage set off his habiliments to the best advantage, would not have betrayed a single external mark of rusticity to the most practised metropolitan eye.

Absorbed and even bewildered as he had been by the recent agitation of his feelings, by the startling change in his life, and a succession of engrossing and strange objects since his arrival in London, he had not omitted to write a most affectionate letter to his mother, for his heart incessantly smote him when he referred to the clandestine mode of his departure from home. With a remorseful yearning, he now wished that he had embraced her, and received her parting blessing, before he left Woodcote; but as it was too late to recall the past, he could only resolve to make such atonement as yet remained in his power, by frequently writing, and imparting to her, in full confidence, all his future plans and prospects.

Although he had procured, and diligently studied, a map of London, his purpose of calling on the Lums—an enterprise which he determined to prosecute on foot—was not so easily executed as he had anticipated. Paris is only half the size of London, yet the French have bestowed double the pains taken by the English in guiding strangers through the labyrinth of their capital. Not only is it divided into compartments, which are so notified in every conspicuous place as to indicate at the same time the points of the compass, but, the odd and even numbers of the houses being appropriated to opposite sides of the streets, much trouble is saved to the passengers, and the risk of accidents from crossing among the crowded carriages is proportionably diminished. These facts may be deemed too notorious to need a record, but it is only by constant harping upon the advantages of any improvement, however slight, that we can eventually procure its adoption.

Not until after many wanderings and numerous inquiries did Allan finally make his way to Great Russell Street, Bloomsbury, when he found that Mr. Lum occupied a handsome-looking house, whereof the ground-floor windows were covered with notices of estates and town and country residences to be let or sold,—the whole copied out in such a large fair round hand that they seemed almost to arrest the passenger's eye and compel perusal. Resisting this temptation, he knocked at a side door, on which was modestly inscribed the word Lum,—the fuller designation and calling of that individual being displayed over the window, in the words "Jonas Lum, Surveyor, Appraiser, and House Agent." Formerly the word "Auctioneer" had been added, but at the earnest solicitation of his daughters, who had an insuperable objection to the hammer, he had consented, when the house-front was last painted, to omit that obnoxious finale,—a sacrifice the less regretted as he flattered himself that the fact of his proficiency in that department needed not any additional publicity.

Most wielders of the hammer, compelled to say a great deal about nothing, and habituated, in what may be literally termed "knock-down aguments," to have all the talk to themselves, acquire a certain confidence and fluency, until, like the celebrated Mr. Puff, they have "as much to say upon a ribbon as a Raphael." But such was by no means the case with Mr. Lum, a tall stiff, starch, pragmatical man, who, having written two or three papers for the Antiquarian's Magazine, deemed himself the Thomas Hearne of Bloomsbury; affecting a certain degree of reserve, and speaking with an oracular solemnity among those of his own class, though he could be obsequious and loquacious enough to his customers.

Ill news may fly apace, but its course is not so rapid, in these anti-connubial times, as the good news which announces that a young bachelor, who had previously been deemed a detrimental, has suddenly become a desirable. Knowing that the narrow circumstances of the Latimers would be still further straitened at the death of the mother, Mr. and Mrs. Lum, keeping studiously aloof from all communication with them, had lost no opportunity of vituperating the folly and pride of the young men, who, with hardly salt to their porridge, chose to lead an idle life, and set up for gentlemen, under the shallow pretext of devoting their time to their sick mother. No sooner, however, had they learnt, upon what they deemed unquestionable authority, that Allan had been adopted by a rich, old, retired merchant at Woodcote, who meant to leave him all his fortune, than they bethought them, with a truly parental anxiety, of their four unmarried daughters, and at the same time felt an affectionate yearning towards the eldest son of their good friends at Woodcote.

"After all," as Mrs. Lum very justly and feelingly observed, "flesh and blood *is* flesh and blood; and though we are so distantly connected that I hardly know how to make it out, I have always felt a real regard for those Latimers." As the husband's feelings were equally kind and cordial, it was mutually resolved to seek some early opportunity of renewing the acquaintance, though neither of them could immediately suggest a feasible mode of accomplishing this object. Great therefore was the delight as well as the surprise of both, when fate, as if for the purpose of anticipating their wishes, brought the object of all their disinterested solicitude to their very door.

On a small circular table of the unoccupied drawing-room, into which Allan was ushered, stood a model of Stonehenge, and of the Cornish Logan or rocking-stone executed in cork; and in the glass-case of a recess were arranged, with explanatory labels of very elaborate penmanship, iron and stone celts, fragments of rusty weapons, large iron rings, rudely-carved round stones, and other rubbishy-looking odds and ends, the original purport of which, had an antiquarian ever suffered himself to be at a loss, it would have been impossible even to surmise. The loo-table in the centre of the room was of solid structure, or it could hardly have supported the three or four volumes of the Antiquarian's Magazine, with all their heavy contents, which were placed upon it.

Upon taking up one of these ponderous tomes, Allan found that it opened spontaneously at a paper signed "Druidicus;" he tried a second, a third, and a fourth, with exactly the same result;—a mystery, of which he was endeavouring to divine the cause, when Mr. Lum walked very uprightly into the room, welcoming his visitant with as much cordiality as if he came to employ him in the purchase or sale of a large estate, and making most particular and tender inquiries concerning the health of his excellent mother and his worthy brother.

"You are an antiquarian, I perceive," said Allan, after exchanging a few similar interrogatories and greetings.

"You *perceive,* Sir?" ejaculated Lum, glancing reproachfully at the magazines. "Surely you must have been previously aware of that fact. Doubtless, you *must* have heard that I am the Druidicus of the Antiquarian's Magazine; for I think I have understood that you are fond of literature."

"Very, but I do not recollect to have heard—I have not been so fortunate as to have read any of the papers so signed." The countenance of the antiquary fell; but as the hopes of the father-in-law *in futuro* sprung up afresh in his heart, one of his least solemn smiles regained the ascendency of his features, and he resumed, "Allow me to repeat, that I should have thought you *must* have heard of the letters of Druidicus, although Woodcote is such a retired place. However, I can lend you one of the volumes. It shall be that which contains my celebrated essay 'On the Shape of the Handle of the Pruning-knife of the Chief Priest, with which he cut the Sacred Mistletoe.' That paper you are sure to like, for I may say, without vanity, that for deep research, and profound interest, and skilful treatment,—however, it does not become me to repeat all that I hear from all the world. But here comes Mrs. Lum. My dear, this is Mr. Latimer, Mr. Allan Latimer, your relation, you know, from Woodcote."

"And I'm sure I'm mons'ous glad to see him," replied the wife, a short, vulgar, corpulent, over-dressed, under-educated woman, who, as she glided about without showing her feet, her petticoats touching the ground, the better to conceal her thick ankles, might have been taken for the original 'fillet of veal upon castors.' "And in course" she continued, "I *must* be glad to welcome my own kith and kin, as a body may say,

Curious enough, ar'nt it, Jonas, that only t'other day I was a sayink, Well, I should be glad, says I, to see one of those nice young men up in Lonnon; and for the matter of that, your mother, too, would have been as welcome as the flowers in May,—for I've no notion, not I, of separating families. Now Mr. L., he likes dinink out, uncommon; but, 'cept to the Freemasons' and public dinners, I don't suffer him to go without I'm asked—do I, dear? No, says I, when he's asked alone, you must cut fair, and take us as we come, fat and lean, lean and fat: ha, ha, haw:"

Allan expressed his acknowledgments for her intended hospitality towards himself and his family, though this was the first intimation he had received of it.

"La! now, only to think!" resumed the lady, who was not less voluble than voluminous; "I quite forgot to 'pologise for keeping you so long a waitink for me, but I was thrown into such a tribilation when I heard the double knock, a'most flabbergasted, as the man says in the play; for between you and I and the post, Mr.

Latimer, Saturdays is always our day for routing out the house, for I can't bear filth, and London ar'nt like the country, you know, so we're obliged to do it, or else we should be in a pretty mess, in no time; shouldn't we, my dear?"

As the erudite antiquary suffered his strong mind to be swayed by the stronger will of his wife, he gave an invariable acquiescence when thus appealed to, although upon the present occasion he did venture to hint that Mr. Latimer might not wish to be let into the confidence of all her domestic arrangements. "Don't tell me, Mr. L.," was the reply, "I know what I'm about; if Mr. Latimer won't think me presumpshous for saying so. If I hadn't told him it was cleaning day, how should he have known why our gals are so long a-comink? You see, Sir, we have given them a good edication, better, a pretty sight, than ever their mother had afore 'em; but though Mr. L., thank God, is well to do in the world—better, I may say, than most of his neighbours, and therefore it's no objick to us—I wish 'em to be brought up- to make good housewives when they marry. They all play the piano, and;' Cilla, my eldest, she sings uncommon pretty; but la! if there should come a rainy day, they won't make the pot boil by strumming a| piano, or working a worsted poll-parrot staring his eyes out at a butterfly or a cabbage-rose; or knitting pusses when they've got nothink to put in 'em,—so my gals have been taught to make their own clothes when they're new, and vamp 'em up when they're old, and darn stockings, and cut out shirts for their father and their brother Tom, and even wash and iron their own collars and tippets, and handkerchers and aperns, and such like: this has been our course of edication; hasn't it, my dear?"

Not wishing to express any opinion upon so undignified a subject, and afraid of appearing discourteous to one who was in every sense his better half, Mr. Lum pretended not to have heard her, and busied himself in selecting the magazine which he meant to lend to his visitant. Observing, however, that the good housewife was occupied in fastening back the window-curtains, to protect them from the sun, Mr. Lum requested his visitant to notice that in the arrangement of his curiosities everything presented an appropriate character; the table that supported the models being circular, the favourite mystic figure of the Druids; the case being made of oak, the tree under whose boughs they always celebrated their rites; and the carved ornament at top representing the sacred mistletoe.

"And may I inquire," asked Allan, "what is contained within these wooden doors, at the lower part of the case?" Drawing himself up to his full height, assuming a mysterious look, and speaking in a solemn whisper, the expanded house-agent replied, "You may certainly **ask,** Sir, nor shall I refuse to gratify so natural and even laudable a curiosity; but as to my showing you what is deposited within, no power on earth shall compel me to it: it would be contrary to my vow of office. I am not a proud or vain man, Mr. Latimer; in many respects, at least in some, I am well aware that I possess no great superiority over my neighbours, but I cannot repress some little degree of exultation when I state that you see before you the Master of the Druids' Lodge of free and accepted Masons! Nay, Sir, I require no marks of respect and homage It **here,**—none whatever," here the speaker looked condescendingly pompous—"not even when I inform you, that in this locked-up case are contained the Regalia, the Respect Board, the decorations, and all the emblematic insignia of my illustrious office."

Allan congratulated him on the dignities he had attained, and hearing at that moment the giggling of female voices outside the door, he expressed a hope that he should see some of the young ladies before he left the house. "Some of them, I have no doubt, will shortly present themselves," replied the father; "but I have four, Sir, four, all good and charming girls; but being Saturday, a busy day with us, as Mrs. L. has already intimated, I fear they may not all be able to appear." As he omitted to specify how the charms which he had assigned to his daughters were respectively apportioned, it may be well to state, that in order to prevent quarrels among themselves, the young ladies had agreed that each should adopt some appropriate excellence, which was to be considered her own exclusive property, and not to be questioned or rivalled by any of the others. Priscilla, the eldest, being the least good-looking, with a cast in one of her eyes, set up for cleverness; Jemima, who was all ringlets and romance, took the sentimental and lackadaisical department; Amelia, laced in till she could hardly breathe, claimed the good figure of the family; and Harriet, who promised to rival her mother in fatness, piquing herself upon her fair skin, and the dimples not only in her cheeks, but in her shoulders and elbows had a charter for going more décolletée than any of her sisters, and always wore short sleeves.

As the two latter, busied, when Allan called, in the discharge of their Saturday duties, were in such complete deshabille as not to admit of their dressing in time to see their visitant, only Priscilla and Jemima, who had made a flurried toilette for the purpose, presented themselves in the drawing-room, which they entered with timid awkwardness, dropping a cold half-curtsey to Allan, seating themselves with an air of constraint on the edge of their chairs, and answering the questions or observations addressed to them with a monosyllabic brevity. Many girls, especially those unaccustomed to society, though hoydening and loquacious enough among themselves, will freeze into an unsocial shyness before a single stranger. But this was not so much the cause of the embarrassment exhibited by the young ladies in question, as the repressive influence of the father, who indemnified himself for his subjection to his wife, by exercising such a rigorous and morose authority over his children, that they were always reserved and generally silent in his presence. Mrs. Lum, however, was always ready to do the talking for the whole family, at the shortest notice and on the most reasonable terms. Having placed herself at the window, after the adjustment of the curtains, she suddenly ejaculated, "There goes Lady Trumpington's carriage, a-drivink to the Museum, I 'spose. Only to see how that vain old 'ooman does rouge! She wants to pass herself off for fat, fair, and forty, but she won't succeed, I don't think, for I'm told she don't want but one year of being sixty. How she can keep that fine carridge, without ever a shillink in her puss, I can't conceive for the life of me, unless it's all done by gambolling, for they do say she plays cards all day Sunday. Mussy on us! if there was to be such wicked doinks in my house, I should expect that some Sabbath night, just as it was a-going to strike twelve, and I was a scorink up the odd trick, I should hear Belzebub himself crying out———"

The conclusion of the sentence was prevented by another voice exclaiming, in a hollow and mysterious whisper, "You're wanted down below;" an announcement which occasioned Allan to start up in some alarm, for the sound seemed to proceed from the wainscot, close to his right ear. An irrepressible shout of laughter from Mrs. Lum, and a giggle from the girls, soon assured him that the words he had heard were not of diabolical origin.

"Well, I declare!" panted the former, quite out of breath with her cachinnations, "was there ever anything so curious as that? Only to see how funnily odds and ends, and tops and bottoms, do come together! Rayley, it's a'most enough to frighten some people out of their wits; but you're in no joppardy, Mr. Latimer, so you may sit down again, without any fear of a call from old Nick; ha, ha, haw!"

"It is doubtless Sir Barnaby Briggs, respecting the house in the square," said the husband; "I expected him about this hour:" and so saying, he stalked out of the room, preserving the same unaltered solemnity of his visage; for it did not become the Master of the Druids' Lodge to laugh, or even to smile. "You see, Sir," resumed his spouse, "Jonas is in the habit of sittink up here, writing his antiquary papers, and what not, for he can't 'bide being bothered when he's a-thinkink, no more he didn't ought, for he don't often do it, and so an iron pipe let into the wall goes right into the counting-house, that he may call down for anything he requires, and that Tom may call up to him when his father's wanted below. It's uncommon convenient, arn't it?"

"A very ingenious contrivance, but rather startling to a stranger," replied Allan.

"It arn't the fust time, by a good many, that people have been took in by it, and frightened, wuss than you was. Did you ever hear the story of Mrs. Alderman Tubbs? La, no; how should ye? It's a rare good 'un, I promise ye. Mrs. Alderman Tubbs, you see, she came to me for the character of a cook, who had just left us, and she sot, just as you may be a-doing now, with her ear close to the pipe. But, says she, '*can* Susan Crump,' (that was the name of the cook,) '*can* she make good fish-sauce? for I've hardly met with one that doesn't ile the butter in melting it. Now, I myself,' says she, 'am uncommon petiklar about my melted butter, and as to my husband the alderman—' Well, Mr. Latimer, before ever she could get out another word, Tom bawls up, through the pipe, right into her right ear, 'He's a dirty, drunken, good-for-nothing feller;' for you see, Tom had been sent to inquire the character of a porter, who came to be hired, and he was to let his father know directly he came in. Wasn't it a curious conjunction? Well, what with the fright, and what with the supposed insult to the alderman, Mrs. Tubbs, she gave sich a scream, and became asterical; but that's not the worst on't, for instead of the little bottle of thieves' vinegar, I snatched up the markink ink, and held it so close to her nose, that I smeared it all over. And now it was my turn to be frightened, for in a minute or two I said, says I, 'Lor a mussy! for certain sure she's a-going to die, for she's a-turning black in the face!' So I rang the bell, and shouted Help! Help! so loud, that it brought her to her senses again as pert as a pearmonger, and in runs Tom to know what the row was about, and when I told him, and he saw her nose kiver'd with ink, he laughed till I really thought he'd a-bust."

The whole gelatinous rotundity of the loquacious dame undulated responsively to her own hearty laugh, at the conclusion of which she hastily collected her breath, and resumed, "But I was uncommon sorry for the accident, for she drove up in her own carridge to the private door, and that always looks well, for in course people wasn't to know she came about the character of a servant. There now, Mr. Latimer, I was a-telling you, ye know, what a good manager my 'Cilla is. Would you ever think that silk gownd was a turn'd 'un? Fact, as I'm sitting here; and, what's more, last week she dropped ever so much mustard—'Cilia's uncommon fond of mustard—upon the front breadth, (served her right, and so I told her, for not wearing her black apern,) and got every atom of it out with French chalk and a bit of flanning. To think of the wear she has had out of that gownd, and it only cost two-and-fourpence a yard at fust."

"La! Ma!" cried the wearer of this enduring article, who had been actively using her eyes since her father left the room, though her mother had monopolized all the talk, "what can Mr. Latimer know or care about silk dresses?"

"That's a pretty thing too, arn't it, that yaller Swish musling of Jemima's,—that's my taste, and I think it becomes her, 'specially with that band, 'cause yeller and laylock goes so well together."

Emboldened by the absence of her father, Priscilla now took her full share in the conversation, frequently talking at the same time as her mother, as she rattled away about the Regent's Park, and the Zoological Gardens on a Sunday, and the Islington Assembly, and the Adelphi Theatre, for which they often got orders, through a friend who was one of the actors, and the Museum, in visits to which (the admission bong gratuitous, and no coach-hire necessary) they were frequently indulged by their parents. During this colloquy, her sister, stealing furtive glances through a whole weeping-willow of corkscrew ringlets, but saying nothing, peered at Allan, and instantly cast down her eyes when she was detected, and sighed, and palpitated, and threw herself into a lackadaisical attitude, with a coquetishness that was meant to appear exceedingly bashful and interesting, until her manœuvres were interrupted by Priscilla's exclamation of "La! Jemy,"—such was the endearing but somewhat masculine abbreviation of her name,—"don't sigh so, or Mr. Latimer will fancy you're in love."

"Answer for yourself, 'Cilla," cried the mother, rather sharply, "and don't snub your sister; for you know, poor thing! she was always given to dumps and doldrums, ever since she was a babby, and used to cry, without any call, when I was a-nussing of her. Is any thing the matter with you, child?"

"Nothing in the world, dear Ma; only I have just finished reading the most heart-rending novel that ever drowned the pitying reader in floods of tears,—'Sympathy and Sentiment, or the Sorrows of Victorine.' Good heavens! what miseries were endured by that victim of sensibility!" With clasped hands, the weeping willow threw up her eyes, fixed them on the hook in the centre of the ceiling, which would have supported a lamp, had there been one, again lowered them to the ground, suffered her hands to fall listlessly upon her lap, and gave a tender sigh.

"Stuff and nonsense!" exclaimed the mother: "it's well your father don't know you read such trash, or he'd chuck it right into the fire."

Can this be the girl, thought Allan, whom I heard giggling and chattering outside the door, notwithstanding all the sorrows of Victorine?

"Gals will have different ways with 'em," said the mother; "now my eldest, she's as merry as a grig, always was. Come, 'Cilla dear, 'spose you cheer us up a bit with a song; not that dismal ditty of the crazy gal in the mad'us, but something funny—'The Musical Wife' or 'The Old Maid' or 'Sweet Jenny Jones' like they sing in the farces."

"Pa don't allow us to sing Italian or French," said Priscilla, seating herself at the instrument; "he thinks it highly improper: but I'm not going to accommodate Ma with any of her comic vulgarities that she's so fond of." She accordingly sang 'Sweet Home,' with some little huskiness in her throat, but with a great deal of expression in her eye, which was immovably and tenderly fixed upon Allan during the whole performance. As this, however, was the truant orb, which indulged in a little obliquity of vision, there might not have been any design either in its direction or expression. Their visitant's confession, that he was himself a vocalist, occasioned an eager petition from the whole trio that he would favour them with a song; Priscilla urging, very strenuously, that she had a right to call upon him; and he accordingly sang two or three English ballads (for he had the fear of the solemn Jonas before his eyes), which were received by his auditors with unbounded delight and applause.

His visit having now been protracted to an almost unreasonable length, he took his leave, but not until he had promised Mrs. Lum that he would dine with them on the following Wednesday. Scarcely had he reached the corner of the street when, hearing hasty footsteps, he looked round, and saw the Master of the Druids' Lodge running after him (almost the only time he was ever known to break out of a walk), bearing the promised volume of the magazine, which Allan took with many apologies for having forgotten to claim it, and pursued his way.

CHAPTER V.

No sooner had their visitant left the house than Mrs. Lum waddled down stairs to inform her husband of the invitation she had given, and to advise with him concerning the parties who should be bidden to the feast; and no sooner were the father and mother thus engaged, than their five children assembled in the drawing-room, to talk over the all-important subject of their new acquaintance, or, as they were now proud to call him, their relation, not without a distant hope, on the part of more than one of them, that he might be still more closely connected with the family.

"What a beautiful man!" cried Amelia, who had hastily thrown on a dressing-gown that she might join in the chat.

"How do *you* know? You never saw him," said Jemima.

"Didn't I, though? I know better than that, Jemy, for when I heard the double knock, I ran to the top of the stairs, and watched him all the way up; and what's more, when I found it impossible to be dressed in time, I crept down in my petticoat to the drawing-room door, and peeped through the keyhole."

"La! 'Mely," objected the eldest sister, with a reproving frown; "how very indelicate! Suppose Pa or Tom had seen you?"

"Oh! I should have skipped back again, four stairs at a time, when I heard any one moving."

"And not one of you told me that he was here; you nasty, spiteful things, you!" exclaimed Harriet, swelling and colouring with vexation.

"Why, you know, dear Harriet," coaxed Jemima, in a soft and soothing voice, "it would have been no use telling you, when you hadn't half done your darning, and had got your hair in papers."

"And why am I to have all the darning, and washing, and ironing of gloves and ribbons? I'm sure one might as well be Cinderella. I'm quite a drudge, and it's a shame; that's what it is!"

Not only was Harriet fat, but she was so large and masculine in her figure, that her brother Tom had given her the nickname of Harry the Boatswain, or, to use his own pronunciation, the Bo'son; in accordance with which unfraternal habit, he only noticed her statement of grievances, pathetic as it was, by exclaiming, "Bo'son Harry seems to be in a passion;" and then, recurring to the subject of Allan, he continued, "I had a famous squint at him,—No, the squint's in' Cilla's department."

"None of your impudence, Mr. Saucebox," snapped Priscilla; "nothing so vulgar as personal remarks,—and besides they come with a very bad grace from such a redheaded Rufus as you!"

"Draw it mild, 'Cilla!" resumed the brother, making a hideous mouth at her. "Well, I was going to say that as soon as I heard the double knock I ran to the counting-house window, and stared at the gentleman all the time that I held my nose to the glass."

"Then I'm sure it wasn't a looking-glass," cried' Cilla, laughing heartily at her own joke.

"And I must say," resumed Tom, in a great hurry, as he was not provided with an immediate retort, "that a better-looking or more stylishly dressed chap I never saw. His coat is the regular go among the tip-top swells—made by Diedrichson—I can swear to the cut—and spic and span new."

"And how charmingly he sings!" added Jemima. "Oh how enviable, how blissful a fate to wander with that man by the side of some translucent stream, silvered by the moonbeams, while the ringdove coos from the eglantine, and the nightingale pours her love-song from the grove!"

"Bravo, Jemy!" sneered the brother; "what a pretty bit of pastoral! Pity you were not born a shepherdess, with a crook in your hand." The sisters smiled, but Jemima, looking still more pensive, and heaving a deep sigh, continued,—

"And *did* you notice his small white hand? Heavens! *what* a hand for putting on the wedding-ring!"

"I find from his conversation," said Priscilla, "that his mother keeps a carriage!" The whole party immediately became silent, looking at one another with an awe-struck and yet complacent expression.

"And it is certain," pursued Tom, "that he has been adopted by a rich old fellow at Woodcote, who means to make him his heir. What a catch!"

"What a catch!!" repeated Priscilla.

"What a catch!!!" echoed Jemima.

"What a catch!!!" re-echoed Amelia, keeping up the *crescendo* tone of amazement.

"And I have never seen him!" sobbed Harriet, bursting into tears.

"Here's a rig!" cried Tom; "the Bo'son's blubbering!" There was something so ludicrous in the phrase, as well as in the appearance of the great overgrown weeping girl, that her companions burst into a simultaneous laugh, whereat Harriet became so deeply incensed, that she snatched up the hearth-brush, and would probably have given some of them cause to remember the weight of the "Bo'son's" arm, had they not suddenly dispersed, and fled giggling to their respective rooms.

"Now, my dear Jonas!" said Mrs. Lum to her husband, both being seated in consultation; "as there's no knowing what may come of this lucky visit,—for Mr. Latimer looked uncommon sweet upon 'Cilla, and it would be sich an objick to him, as he's so fond of music, to get a gal that sings,—I must confess I should like to make a favourable impression upon him."

"Quite right, quite right, Mrs. L.; but I flatter myself that I have already succeeded in that object, for I have apprized him that I am master of the Druids' Lodge, and I have lent him the volume of the Magazine which contains——"

"Psha! never mind that! I was a thinkink of our dinner-party—who we should ask so as to let him see that we've a genteel set of acquaintance,—and we had better settle the pint at once; 'cause, if we're too long about it, we shan't have time enough. Now, the genteelest people we know, out and out,—because they're the richest, and have got a country-house at Hackney, and drive a four-wheel shay of their own,—is the Snodgrasses,—but then they keep a shop."

"True, Mrs. L., but it's one of the most thriving haberdashers' in London, and you forget that Mr. Snodgrass is a Freemason, though not a master."

"Still he keeps a shop,—which, somehow or other, sticks in my gizzard uncommon—that's to say, 'cause it might stick in Mr. Latimer's. Now, what think you of Mr. Snaggs, the dentist, and his wife? He's in the profession, you know; in course we should say he was a surgeon, which always sounds well; and he's sich a funny man,—quite a wag; and Mrs. Snaggs, she **must** be a genteel 'ooman, for she's a niece, you know, of Sir Matthew Mumpisson, the City knight, who was once Lord Mayor. In short, Jonas, I've made up my mind to have them."

"I should particularly wish you to invite Mr. and Mrs. Snaggs," said the husband, with the air of a man laying down the law, though he was receiving and obeying it.

"Well, Jonas; then I shall ask the two Popkinses, the clerks in the Museum, or, as we should say, officers of the Museum, for that word always sounds well, don't it? 'cept a sheriffs officer,—that's no go; ha, ha, ha! Mr. Popkins he's wonderful clever, though some people think him sich a prig,—and then he has got all the hard words in the Museum by heart; and Nic, Tom's friend, is a smart dashy young chap, and seems uncommon disposed to cast a sheep's eye at our Amelia, for he gave her a brooch t'other day, with a bleeding heart right in the middle of it; and I do suspect that she's a nettink of a puss for him upon the sly. Now our dining-room won't 'commodate no more than ten,—that is, not to have elber-room,—and that'll be jist it. You and I, and the two eldest gals, and Tom, makes five; and the two Snaggses is seven; and the two Popkinses is nine; and Mr. Latimer jist makes ten percisely."

"You're quite right, Mrs. L., quite: I see you understand my wishes perfectly, and I shall leave all the arrangement of the dinner to you; for with so many more important matters upon my mind, it can hardly be expected——"

"In course not—you've no call to trouble your head about it. I shall talk that over with 'Cilla, who has got quite a genus for cookery, and indeed is petiklar clever, I may say, in all the fine arts."

Great and general were the bustle and commotion in the Lum family in preparing for such an unusual occurrence as a grand dinner-party; grave and manifold were the consultations of the two elder sisters as to what they should wear; deep the heartburning of the juniors when they learnt that they were only to make their appearance at the tea-table. Amelia, whose mind matched her narrow waist, who was, moreover, an artful and forward girl, and vain enough of her figure to believe that she must inevitably make a conquest of Allan Latimer if she were only allowed fair play, determined, if possible, to get a seat at the dinner-table, notwithstanding the cruel interdict that had shut her out. Well knowing that her mother "ruled the roast," her first pathetic appeal was in that quarter, and, when this met with a decided negative, she resolved to try the effect of a little cajolery upon the father, to whose besetting foible she was no stranger.

"How, 'Mely," frowned the Freemason as he was passing up to his own room at a late hour; "not in bed yet? This is wrong, very wrong; I cannot allow such a waste of coals and candle."

"Pray, pray, dear papa!" petitioned' Mely coaxingly, "let me sit up ten minutes longer, that I may finish the third reading of your last paper in the 'Antiquary's Magazine.' It *is* so learned, and *so* deep, and so *very* interesting."

"Well, well, child!" replied "Druidicus," patting her head condescendingly, and almost smiling; "be it so; since I find you're so well employed, and not wasting your time."

"You know, pa, I could talk to Mr. Latimer all about this paper, and those in the volume you lent him, if I were only to dine at table next Wednesday."

"So you could, so you could. I'll speak to your mother about it. Good night, dear!" As the mother continued inexorable, notwithstanding this sudden outburst of antiquarian enthusiasm,' Mely, rendered desperate, had recourse to an ungenerous trick, which, it is to be hoped, nothing but the extremity of the occasion could have provoked. Jemima (she of the ringlets and romance) possessed but one dress gown in a wearable state, and a very smart one it was, being a book muslin, with red ribbons drawn through the tucks, to match the sash and streamers of the same colour. After fifty alterations the weeping willow of corkscrew curls had received its last spiral touch, and Jemima, looking complacently back at the glass as she receded from it, advanced to the closet to take down the dress, which, after a vigilant inspection, she had that very morning hung tenderly upon the peg with her own hands, when a piercing scream that echoed through the house announced some dire catastrophe. Loud as it was, it was scarcely equal to the enormity of the occasion, for lo! the gown—the *only* dress gown—was lying on the closet-floor, completely soused and discoloured with dirty water, which appeared to have proceeded from an overturned washhand-basin beside it.

"That horrid cat!" exclaimed Amelia, running in and contemplating the mishap with a look of infinite amazement and dismay; "she's always doing some mischief."

"Oh,' Mely!' Mely!" sobbed her sister, who had thrown herself into a chair, with as much despairing self-abandonment as was consistent with the careful and becoming disposition of her ringlets; "malignant fate ever darts its most poisonous arrows into the tenderest and most sensitive heart! I am the victim of a conspiracy—the martyr of some diabolical plot. Could a cat take down the dress from its peg, or place the washhand-basin in the closet, or upset it so very carefully over the gown so is as to drench it so completely? No, no; it u has been done on purpose, by some base as: assassin, some vile incendiary, some fiend in a human form."

"Well, Jemy, it can't be helped now, however it may have happened, and you must make up your mind not to appear at table, for it's almost dinner-time, and you've got no other dress, you know. I must run and tell ma of this shocking accident; I dare say she'll be frightened at your scream,—and to be sure it was ridiculous enough for such a trifle." With these words the treacherous' Mely, who had pinched in her waist to its very smallest dimensions, and made her toilet beforehand, so as to be quite ready for the anticipated emergency at the very shortest notice, ran from the room to communicate the disaster to her parents, which she did in such a manner as very seriously to compromise the cat. At that busy and anxious moment there was no time for investigation; Jemima and the cat—for the absent are always wrong—were blamed for their negligence, with an additional and very sagacious remark on the part of Mrs. Lum, "that there wasn't a mischeevouser animal in the world than a cat, when it had once made up its mind to *be* mischeevous;" and as the bearer of the tidings was seen to be ready dressed á quatre épingles, she was desired to take her sister's place,—an order which she immediately obeyed by securing a chair in the drawing-room next to that which she thought most likely to be occupied, on his arrival, by Mr. Latimer.

Meanwhile, as Jemima, brooding over her miseries, adverted to' Mely's instant accusation of the cat, which had all the appearance of being premeditated,—to the circumstance of her being ready dressed so much before her time,—and the galling fact of her having been actually invited by her parents to take her place at the dinner-table, which she presently learnt from Harriet,—it suddenly flashed across her indignant mind that the whole must have been a treacherous and wicked plot for the express purpose of supplanting her with the white-handed and handsome heir of

the rich old merchant. The desire of vengeance instantly succeeding to this conviction, she flew to' Mely's drawer, ferreted out from its six silver-paper wrappings her
favourite brooch, the gift of Nic Popkins, and smashed it beneath her heel,—tore
into little bits an ardent and encomiastic valentine immeasurably valued because it
was suspected to have been the production of the aforesaid Nic,—broke into three
pieces a slate-pencil, which was preserved as a relic because the same party had gal-
lantly cut a point to it with his own knife;—snipped to rags the silken purse whose
intended destination she had always strongly suspected,—carefully replaced all the
fragments in the drawer,—returned to her own room, and endeavoured to solace
herself by anticipating 'Mely's rage when she should discover the mischief, and by
perusing 'Love and Suicide,' a high flown sentimental novel which she had furtively
smuggled into the house.

While this domestic tragedy was enacting up-stairs, the rest of the family, ex-
cepting its master, were collected in the drawing-room, all tricked out in their very
hest, sitting very stiffly upright for fear of deranging their dress, beginning to feel
very nervous as the dinner-hour approached, and quarrelling among themselves
(for want of any better subject) as to who was likely to come first.

"What a bore!" cried Tom; "they have got the pavement up in Charlotte Street,
just the way that the Snaggses will come. I told the fellows we had a grand dinner-
party coming, and they promised to have the stones down again by five o'clock,—
but I doubt it. 'Cilla dear! I wish you'd just look round the corner with your squint
eye—you needn't leave your chair—and see whether the pavement's all smooth."

Endeavouring to dart an angry glance at the utterer of this impertinence,
though one of her orbs *would* look quite away from him, Priscilla tartly exclaimed,
"How many times must I tell you that mine is not a squint, which looks inward, but
a cast, which looks outward, and which many people think a great beauty?'

"Do they? then you had better keep it by all means, for it's the only one you've
got," rejoined the brother.

"And how many beauties have *you* got, I wonder, besides your red hair?"—
This altercation was fortunately checked by the entrance of "Druidicus," whose
austere manners were generally a bar to conversation, except upon the part of himself and his wife; and shortly afterwards the company began to arrive, all punctual
as the clock, for people who are not often invited to a good dinner never run the

risk of spoiling it by exceeding the appointed hour.

"What a very curious coincidence!" said Mrs. Lum; "I said Mr. Latimer would come first—and here he is! Well, I dare say all the others will be here immegently, if nothink don't happen to purvent' em." This safe augury being soon accomplished, Allan had the honour of being introduced to Mrs. Snaggs, as "the niece of Sir Matthew Mumpisson;" to Mr. Snaggs, "a gentleman of the profession;" and to Mr. Popkins and Mr. Nicholas Popkins, "officers of the Museum." Dinner being shortly afterwards announced,—for the master of the house enforced a rigid punctuality in all things,—he handed down the niece of Sir Matthew, who was of course entitled to precedence; Allan, at the instance of her mother, took charge of Priscilla; Popkins senior, having first taken off his spectacles, wiped them, and put them in their case, and the case in his pocket, offered his arm to Amelia; and Tom brought up the rear with his friend Nic Popkins, whom he took by the tip of his little finger and handed down with a mock ceremony, though he thought his attitude so graceful that he could not help looking at the glass as he strutted out of the room.

Upon no altar are so many old jokes offered up to Momus as upon a dinner-table, where, as the risible and edible propensities excite each other, a small jest often provokes a great laugh, and every guest, with a sort of inverse ratio gratitude, thinks himself bound to deliver bad things from his mouth, in return for the good things that he puts into it,—a liberty of which the waggish Mr. Snaggs took full advantage on the present occasion, though his jokes were too old and too little of their age to bear transcription into the pages of this history.

"Our friend sets up for a wag," whispered Priscilla to Allan, "but sometimes he is nothing better than a chatterbox. He's a dentist, you know; and I once ventured to tell him, when he was running on in this way, that he held everybody's jaw but his own—Ha! ha!"

"Them are scollop'd oysters," said Mrs. Lum, cataloguing the dishes; "and what answers to' em yonder is a pig's face."

"Then the answer comes before the question," laughed Snaggs, "for I never heard the oysters say a word. I'm not fond of pig's face, so. I'll take a slice of the edge-bone, after all, or rather of the beef, for Mr. Lum might find it difficult to cut the bone thin enough. But no carrots, if you please: I hate carrots."

"Do you hear that?" whispered Priscilla, aside to Tom. "He's not fond of pig's face, and he hates carrots: if you've a grain of politeness, you ought to quit the table instantly." Taking clever advantage of a momentary pause, Mrs. Lum exclaimed, in the intervals of tilting her plate, and ladling up the gravy with a broad-tipped knife,—"I see Lady Trumpington has fresh painted her carriage. I believe your mother's char'ot, Mr. Latimer, is yaller?" Allan silently assented; the visitors looked at him with an increased respect; and Popkins senior, bowing till his chin touched the turkey's protruding leg, and looking very deferential, hoped he might have the honour of taking wine with him. "Here's a famous pidging-pie, and some broccilo to eat with it," said the hostess. "How funny it looks,—don't it?—seeing all the pidgings lying upon their backs, with their claws up in the air, as if they were praying to be let out! And how vexatious that I should have such a poor appetite to-day! but the fact is, I had quite a turn this morning; for I happened to be a passing of the Serpentine jest as they were dragging it for a beautiful young gal that had drownded herself for love; and the boatmen cried out 'We've got the body!' which made me quite qualmish; but when they pulled it up, what should it be but an old Jew clothes-man, with a long beard and three hats on his head? Sich a disappointment! Mr. Popkins," continued the hostess, with a look and tone of excusable triumph in the grandeur of her dinner—"Mr. Popkins, there's apple-pie and tapioco-pudd'n! Mr. Nicholas Popkins, there's custards!—you'll excuse the cups being of different patterns, but my children do break things uncommon, though they're old enough to know better. 'Cilla dear, I won't have you eat any more of the pudd'n; remember how it disagreed with you at our last dinner-party, only a few months ago. Won't nobody take nothink more? I'm afraid you don't like your dinner. Petic'lar poor feeders, to be sure!"

During the repast the elder Popkins and his host had mostly conversed with each other on the subject of the British antiquities in the Museum, while the younger brother had filled Tom with envy by describing a horse he had just bought,—the stable and its occupants being the only subject upon which the latter was competent to maintain a conversation. "Tom!" cried the father, rebukingly—"you talk of nothing but follies and frivolities. I wish you would pay a little more attention to antiquities, and qualify yourself, in my absence, to explain my collection to strangers."

"Well, so I do. When the gentleman asked me the probable use of the iron hoop found in the South Down Barrow, didn't I tell him it must have gone round the wheel of the barrow? I'm not sure that I shan't write a book to prove it, one of these days."

"La, Tom!" cried the mother, "I'm sure nothink that comes out of your head will ever be read."

"Unless some one plucks a hair out of it," exclaimed 'Cilla, laughing heartily at her own sally.

When the wine was placed upon the table, Mrs. Lum, beginning with the niece of Sir Matthew Mumpisson, audibly drank the health of every one present, politely calling the attention of those who did not immediately hear her by repeating their names in a louder key,—an example which was followed by the rest of the family. After two or three rounds of port and sherry, which Priscilla and Amelia, on a significant wink from their mother, respectively declined, the ladies withdrew, and Allan, finding very little attraction in the conversation of his remaining companions, soon followed to the drawing-room, where he found that Harriet, the youngest sister, had been added to the party, in all the full-blown pride of her own plumpness, displayed to the best advantage by a low dress and short sleeves.

"Are we not to have the pleasure of seeing your sister Jemima?" he inquired, addressing himself to Amelia, as he took a chair beside her.

"No; poor dear Jemy has met with a sad accident: our horrid cat has spoiled the dress she meant to wear. That cat ought to be hung. I never was more distressed at anything in all my life. And then only to think of that unfeeling Mr. Snaggs turning the accident into fun, and saying that it was literally a *cata*strophe!"

"I never saw more profuse ringlets than your sister Jemima's; indeed, you have all fine hair: and how nicely Miss Lum's is arranged, particularly behind!"

"What, 'Cilla's? Ah, but consider what an immense advantage she has! With that eye of hers she can see the back of her head just as well as the front. How do you like Nic Popkins? isn't he a smart young man? And he ought to continue a young man all his life, Mr. Snaggs says, for if he doesn't he'll be old Nick. He cuts such a dash in the Park on a Sunday with his tandem!"

"I cannot say that I admire a tandem."

"La! and I think it so stylish. Why, if he had another horse on the side of each of those that he drives, it would be four-in-hand, you know." Mrs. Lum, not by any means approving this flirtation, as she had appropriated Allan to her eldest daughter, found some pretext for calling Amelia away, at the same time making a signal to Priscilla to take her place,—an object which was frustrated by Harriet, who, thinking it high time that she should have a little chat with their handsome visitant, darted into the vacant chair, and maintained the seat she had occupied, in spite of all her mother's frowns, nods, winks, and pointings. The other gentlemen shortly made their appearance, and Harriet was authoritatively ordered to make tea. "This comes of being the youngest," she whispered to Allan—"I am the drudge of the whole family. I hate a party when I don't dine at table, for we have hashed meat or bubble-and-squeak for a week afterwards; and 'pa and 'ma always finish the port and sherry that's left, leaving us nothing but the nasty old ginger-wine. It's such a trouble making tea for so many! I wish you would sit by my side, and help me."

To the great discomfiture of 'Cilla and her mother—for Jemima was evidently making the most of her dimples—Allan did as he was desired. After the tea-things had been removed, he sang two or three times "by particular request," when he patiently went through a severe course of ballads from Miss Lum, who seemed very much disposed to justify her sister's averment as to her vocal interminability. Taking advantage of the first move from the piano, he at length made his bow and left the house, secretly resolving that his acquaintance with the Lum family should never be extended beyond the bounds of common civility.

CHAPTER VI.

THE concert in which Allan had undertaken to play a violoncello accompaniment to Signora Guardia, and which was crowded with persons of fashion and distinction, passed off most successfully, all being enchanted with the wonderful powers and surpassing graces of the beautiful vocalist, while a buzz of female voices ran round the room, inquiring the name of the handsome young stranger who had accompanied her with such admirable skill. Their curiosity was rather excited than allayed by the answers of Crevetti, his only apparent acquaintance, who, in imparting his name, added that he was a gentleman from the country, that his residence in London would be of short duration, and that he had kindly undertaken to attend his pupils so long as he himself should be incapacitated from doing so by the accident to his hand.

Here was a stimulating story to the idlers who are ever thirsting for gossipry and excitement! Allan was a new "Wandering Minstrel,"—a hero in disguise, ay, and in the most interesting of all disguises—that of a remarkably handsome and fashionably dressed young man. As a substitute for Crevetti he was everywhere gladly received—he discharged his delegated duty at several public and private concerts; and, as the Italian's terms were high, he was not less surprised than gratified to find, at the end of the first month, that the moiety of his earnings amounted to no inconsiderable sum. Magnified to his eyes by the economical habits of his previous life and his ignorance of London expenses, it pleased him the more because it afforded him a reasonable prospect of immediate support without withdrawing a single shilling from the family at Woodcote, whose comforts were of much more importance to him than his own.

Isola had kindly requested him to call upon her as often as he found it convenient,—a permission of which he was so glad to avail himself that scarcely a day passed without his seeing her, and never did he leave her presence without a deeper and more heartfelt admiration of her varied graces, her unrivalled gifts and attainments. More than once had he been invited to her evening parties, which were in high repute for their manifold attractions, the all-accomplished hostess not only entertaining her guests with her musical and conversational powers, but occasionally delighting them with improvisations, both serious and comic, upon subjects given by the guests. Here he met a curious medley of London society— peers, members of Parliament, authors, musical performers both amateur and professional, actors and actresses, men of real and of would-be fashion, whose language, manners, minds, and subjects of discourse, all assuming a metropolitan type and character, were either so completely unintelligible to him, or so little in unison with his own principles and sentiments, that, feeling his utter incompetency to mingle in the conversation, he usually sat apart, silent and abashed, though not always unamused.

After Isola's performances, indeed, all other sounds were but as a tinkling cymbal to his ear, all other impressions were unexciting to his heart. He brooded over their memory, absent even in the midst of company, and requiring no other entertainment than his own musing thoughts. Gladly would he have shared the privilege of others, when he saw them thus crowding round to discourse with her; but in such society, whose superiority to himself in colloquial readiness he instantly recognised, he wanted courage and confidence for the attempt. Enough for him if he could pick up an occasional remark or repartee that fell from her lips: enough for him to sit still and wonder at the ever-varying powers of mind with which she adapted herself to her different colloquists, at her perfect ease and self-possession, at her playful vivacity combined with the respect that she evinced for others, and quietly yet decisively exacted in return.

Nor did this latter power of repressing impertinence appear to be superfluous, for more than once had he noticed a rude stare and an impudently leering look in some of the visitants, while he had been an involuntary hearer of whispering insinuations at which he found it difficult to repress his indignation, so completely were they opposed to his own profound reverence of Isola, and his deep conviction of her purity. That such injurious surmises should proceed from parties who were sharing her hospitality, and for whom she was gratuitously displaying her unrivalled talents, appeared an ingratitude not less wicked than cruel and wanton. He had yet to learn that there exists in London a class of profligates who consider a foreigner and an actress, especially if she be lone and unprotected, a fair object for their licentious attacks, and who will not scruple to assail her reputation the more bitterly because they may have failed to undermine her virtue.

With still greater surprise did he learn that some of these parties, who made no secret of their unhallowed aims, were husbands, fathers, men beyond the meridian of life, whose age as well as their position in society rendered their unprincipled designs doubly revolting. Both old and young, however, of this dissipated crew were restrained as well as charmed by the guarded and decorous conduct of Isola, who evinced a spirit and energy that instantly and effectually repressed every attempt, either by word or gesture, at undue familiarity or freedom.

One peculiarity in Isola's demeanour was her almost incessant restlessness, both of person and countenance. Rarely would she sit for many minutes in the same place, and if she did she frequently sank into a sudden reverie, from which she would break into unconscious laughter, or melt into unheeded tears. In one of his morning visits Allan ventured to notice and inquire the cause of this habit. "I will answer no questions," was the smiling reply, "so long as you call me Signora. Are you not my brother? do I not call you Camillo? Why then do you not treat me as a sister?"

"I will do so if I may baptize you afresh from the waters of the Borromean Lake, and not only call you Isola, but Isola Bella."

"I quarrel with nothing but the cold word Signora. Do you ask why I am so restless? Because I am an exile,—because I can neither know peace nor repose in a foreign land,—because my heart, like a dog that has lost his master, cannot remain still, but is ever anxious, ever on the quest, until it finally resolves to turn towards home and seek him there. Incessantly is every one of my senses on the *qui vive* that it may snatch at some association connected with Italy, with Naples, with my native and beautiful Island of Ischia, and the friends I have left behind me. Why have I fitted up this little garden with its flowers, its laurels, and its tiny bay-tree, except to remind me of my home? This tuberose—Camillo's favourite flower—wafts to me a thousand pleasant memories; there is a silent eloquence in its fragrance that is at once perfume and music to my soul. Yonder Psyche is the work of his hands, and, as I gaze at it, I fly back to Italy upon its outstretched wings. You saw me burst yesterday into tears because a yellow butterfly, brought hither, I conclude, by one of the plants, settled upon my hand.—Exactly the same circumstance occurred when I was sitting beside my mother's death-bed at Naples, and methought her spirit had wafted me back that little soul-emblem from the flowers I planted on her grave, as a memorial of her love. You wondered t'other day that I should suddenly spring from my chair, and dance about the room for joy. The tune played by a passing organ had recalled a happy day when I danced to it at Sorrento."

"You seem, indeed, to have a most excitable temperament. I should hardly have thought that trifles so light would have produced such powerful effects upon your imagination and your feelings."

"And why not? A spark setting fire to a train may blow up a citadel or a city; and association, the gunpowder of the mind, may be as easily kindled, and as expansive when inflamed. Looking out upon my little Italian garden, and seeing nothing of the street below, I sometimes imagine the noise and the rumbling of the passing vehicles to be the roar of the storm-chafed Mediterranean, as I have heard it dashing against the rocks of Ischia. London has my body, you see, but my heart and my thoughts are frequently far, far away, amid the myrtle-groves or beside the music-breathing shores of my own beautiful and sunny land,"

"And yet you must have found some pleasure in your English abode, if I may judge by the variety of trinkets and ornaments with which you have decorated your apartment."

"With the exception of this figure of Psyche—the work, as I have already told you, of my dear Camillo—they are all gifts. I am going to run the risk of losing your good opinion—that is to say, if I have already gained it. You will think me mercenary, sordid, perhaps mean-spirited, when I confess to you that, as I came hither, encountering your chilling climate, and not less cold and uncongenial manners, for the sole purpose of making money, I never decline it, never refuse a present—no, not even when I am well aware that the secret motives of the donor would authorise me in considering it an insult. You start, you seem surprised—and I do not wonder; but listen to me, and you will perhaps think me justified.—Among a few friends whom I respect because they respect me, others have sought my acquaintance—have almost thrust themselves into my house, and tender me their insidious flattery and gifts, from motives which I cannot fail to detect, but which, from my unprotected situation, I have not the means to resent as I could wish. By receiving their offerings and rejecting themselves, I can at once punish them and promote my own object, which is the speedy attainment of a certain sum, that I may the sooner return to Italy. I make them pay but a small penalty for the great and grievous wrong they would inflict upon me;—nay, how can they call it a penalty at all? since I never hold out a false hope, but sternly discountenance their advances, and repudiate their homage, even when they are depositing their offerings upon my altar."

"Insolent profligates! I wonder how you can repress your indignation in their presence. And whence comes the calm self-possession with which you receive the compliments of other and very different characters—men of talent and of honour, who respect not less deeply than they admire you? Such flattering tribute might turn the strongest head,—but in you, Isola Bella, I cannot perceive a single trace of vanity, affectation, or coquetry."

"If I am really free from those failings, I can readily explain the cause. I have no small passions; they are all swallowed up in the one master-feeling which has complete dominion of my head, my heart, my soul"

"And what is that?"

"Aha! Camillo mio! would you have me reveal my secret? Not yet, not yet; though I may perhaps divulge it to you before I leave England Of this be assured, that when I do return to Italy I shall carry with me my own respect, a conscience free from reproach, whatever may be thought of me by others. But you must be tired of all this egotism,—and if not, I am. Come, shall I sing to you? Giddy creature that I am! Hark at my three musical clocks all tuning up together to remind me that I have an engagement in Langham Place."

"And to afford me the hope that I may be allowed to escort you."

"May all your hopes be as surely and as speedily accomplished!"

"I am never tired," said Allan, as they pursued their walk, "of admiring this noble promenade, so varied and yet so striking in its whole range from Waterloo Place to the Regent's Park. How immeasurably superior to the barrack-like uniformity of the older streets! The Duke of York's column, however, ought to have been fluted, and ought not to have been *his.* If it means to assert that he performed anything entitling him to the honour of surmounting it, we can only pronounce (as was once said of its brother on Fish Street Hill) that it 'lifts the head, and lies' To bestow such a distinction on such a man is an architectural immorality, a public wrong,—unless, indeed, it may be defended on the principle that unmerited eminence, like praise undeserved, 'is censure in disguise.'"

"Perhaps that may be the Duke's own opinion," smiled Isola, "for you see he turns his back upon us as if he were ashamed to show his face. Yes, I agree with you, there is a beauty, a brilliancy, an expansiveness about this promenade that always charms me. If it was said of ancient Tyre that her merchants were princes, may we not pronounce the shopkeepers of Regent Street to be peers? All the wealth of the four quarters of the world seems poured into it. Look at this window:—how beautiful are these shawls, and what low prices are affixed to them! Nay; I will not stop,—there's nothing so expensive as cheapness; it tempts you to buy, and, as I told you before, I am a money-scraper, not a money-spender. I like, nevertheless, to watch the gazers at the different windows, and the expression of their countenances; it gives an insight into character."

"Mark, Isola, yonder handsome girl,—with what an intense yearning she gloats upon that expensive shawl!"

"Poor creature! she has evidently been led into temptation, and I trust she will be delivered from evil, for there may be eventual shame and suicide in that covetous look."

"Was it not an Athenian saying, that the man who had the fewest wants came the nearest to the gods, who had none?"

"And was it not the Stoics who maintained that the best way to gratify, or rather to prevent your wants, was to suppress your desires, which some wag has compared to the pleasant process of cutting off your legs that you may not require boots? Certain it is, that if we had no ungratified desires we should have a much less vivid enjoyment of existence; for hope is often sweeter than reality. For myself I can answer that my greatest present pleasure is the anticipation of a joy to come."

"The delight, in short, of returning to Italy. Ah, Isola! I cannot share with you in that! Well, I must submit to my fate. Some one says that we may all have what we like by liking what we have; and upon that principle the present moment may perhaps be the happiest of my life, for am I not walking on a fine day, in one of the finest and most amusing streets in Europe, with Isola Bella by my side?"

"Beware, Camillo! It has hitherto been the greatest charm of your society that you have never attempted to flatter me. If you begin to pay me compliments, I shall fancy you are like other men, which, I can assure you, would be no small disadvantage to you. Look at these beautiful horses and splendid carriages, collected opposite a shop-window, whose whole wide expanse, gorgeous and sparkling with gold and jewels, is only protected from the forlorn paupers or daring rogues who gaze at them outside by a piece of glass which a blow would shiver, but which protects them as effectually as if it were an impenetrable wall of brass. Surely this is the very triumph of civilisation."

"And police."

"Which is the same thing. We laugh at the shipwrecked voyager who was so highly gratified at discovering a gibbet where he was washed ashore; but he was right, for it showed him that there were securities for life and property, which is everything."

"Yet it is painful, to me at least, to see the two extremes of wealth and poverty brought together, almost into contact,—as at this gold and jewel flashing window, for instance."

"Nay; these are superfluities—idle luxuries, of which the poor scarcely know the use, and with which the wealthy might well dispense. But look ye here, Camillo! behold these young chimney-sweepers; how ravenously they devour with their eyes the rolls in that pastry-cook's window, while the lounging epicures within are endeavouring to provoke their palled appetites by some stimulating confection."

'Poor little wretches!" said Allan, slipping some money into their hands,—"they shall feast more than their eyes this morning."

"I have seen nothing in England," resumed Isola, "which fills me with a deeper compassion than the sight of these poor Parias and outcasts of society. Ungrateful people that you are! these imps of darkness are your Lares and Penates, your household gods, the guardians of your hearths, the dispensers of comfort and safety to your cherished fire-sides. The very soot that begrimes, and often subjects them to disease, comes from the fires which have roasted your venison, heated your turtle-soup, cheered and enlivened your social circles; and in reward for services which involve constant toil and suffering, and occasional risk of life, you give them a year's destitution with a single May-day's Saturnalia. How you English, who are such preachers of charity and emancipation, can employ these poor victims, when you might safely accomplish the same object by machinery, I cannot understand."

"People are used to the employment of these boys, and do not advert to their sufferings."

"Ah! custom and thoughtlessness are the old excuses for cruelty and oppression. But here I am at my journey's end; this is the house I am to call at Thanks and farewell for the present, and do not forget your promise to meet me at the rehearsal."

"It is little likely to escape my recollection. I will wait for you at the door of the Opera-house."

When Allan had an hour or two to spare, he generally devoted them to a ramble in one or other of the Parks, which, by their amplitude, their verdant beauty, and the noble views they commanded, constituted, in his opinion, the most striking feature and the greatest embellishment of the metropolis. He was making his way towards Hyde Park, after having parted from Isola, when in Oxford Road he was saluted with the exclamation, "Ah! Allan Latimer, my jolly freshman! I am glad to see you. How fare you?—what tidings of Isola?—which way are you wending? *N'importe.* I'm going your way, whatever it may be." And ere Allan could give any answer to this string of interrogatories, he found himself walking arm-in-arm with Harry Freeman, to whom he had been introduced by Isola at her last party, and who had kindly volunteered to act as his Cicerone about London,—an offer of which he had already availed himself, and had been much pleased with his companion.

Harry, who was of no profession, might perhaps be best described as a ***chap*** about town;—a pleasant, lively, rattling ***pococurante.*** Though young and handsome, he was utterly free from coxcombry or vanity; but, on the other hand, although a gentleman by birth and education, his manners and language were sometimes vulgar from an affectation of low buffoonery, slang terms, and ungrammatical language. Passionately fond of singing, and with a voice that could accommodate itself with ease to the most difficult operatic music or the broadest comic song from an English pantomime, he was equally at home in all games, all sports, all recreations, whether social or solitary, rural or civic, high or low, indoors or out of doors, making himself universally welcome by his good humour and his animal spirits, neither of which had ever been known to fail him. When he affected the language, he generally assumed the look, voice, and gestures of the vulgar, all of which he could imitate to perfection. In this, however, as in almost everything else, the outward and the inner man were antitheses to each other; and it was happily said of him that the only character which he never mimicked, and yet never forgot, was that of a gentleman. "You're a precious lucky dog, Latimer!" said Harry, who was as free and easy with his companion as if he had known him for years; "you're in high favour with the Signora, I can tell you that; and there are lots of prime swells in London, top-sawyers, fellows with strawberry-leaves round their coronets, who would give their ears to stand in your shoes."

"I am highly flattered by the Signora's good opinion, but I am not aware that I have done anything to deserve it," said Allan, slightly colouring.

"Well, if you've not, you needn't look like the red lion of Brentford. Confound it! I wish I could blush, though they tell me I did look deuced red when I was had up for that lark at Knightsbridge, and I have ever since had the nickname of the Lobster, because I only turn red when I get into hot water. I spun a regular yarn— had a precious long palaver with the Signora about you yesterday. 'It is such a treat,' she exclaimed,—you know her way of speaking," pursued Freeman, pursing up his mouth and endeavouring to imitate the sweet and gracious tones of the Italian;—"it is such a treat to me, who am constantly beleaguered with roués *and* blasés, men of the town, dandies and debauchees,—palled, and jaded, and insolent creatures, who have worn out their head and heart, and retain nothing but the worst of their senses—it is such a treat to encounter, in a young man who is handsomer and cleverer than the best of them, a fresh, and pure, and unsophisticated spirit—one that is yet unspoiled by the pleasures and vices of London—one who is modest and diffident, though his attainments might well make him vain—a man who can admire me, and yet be afraid to confess it—who, when others are seeking to cajole me by their insidious flattery, can stand apart and blush!—and such a phoenix of a man is Mr. Latimer.' There, my fine fellow! learnt her speech all by heart on purpose for you. I harn't spelled sich a long lesson afore since I left school."

"And don't you think the Signora is rather inconsistent to say I am not vain, while she is thus taking the most effectual means to make me so?" asked Allan, with an assumed carelessness, while his whole frame thrilled with pleasure, not unmixed with a touch of jealous curiosity, as he continued—"But surely you yourself must share her good opinion, since you thus possess her confidence?"

"Oh! she chats familiarly with me, be-cause she knows me to be a safe fellow. I have such a regard for the sex in general that I never flirt with one in particular. I'm rather a queer fish, a rum cove. I play all games, but never for money—attend racecourses, but never bet—lounge in at gaming-houses, but only to look on—talk politics, and don't care a button about them—possess lots of acquaintance (you among the number), but am rather shy of friendships, for friends are always quarrelling; and what's stranger still, and makes Harry Freeman a phoenix, a *rara avis,* a white swan among the black ones, though my income is small, I never exceeds it, and never owes nobody nothink in the whole vide vorld."

"Which, amid so many temptations, shows you to be a man of high principle."

"Don't you be such a flat, such a pancake, such a greenhorn as to fancy that. Principle! deuce a bit. Interest, my hearty; nothing else upon earth. In the choice of evils, I had rather live upon my income than be bothered with duns—that's all. There are two things of which I am particularly fond—singing, and the personal ease of a certain Harry Freeman; but my hobby-horse—my prime swell—my trump card—my bang-up topper in the way of enjoyment, is a certain noun-substantive—

namely, life by itself—life!"

"You seem to have everything, indeed, to make it happy."

"Ay, and I should make it happy, or rather it would make me happy, without anything."

"A pleasant system of philosophy."

"Rather say a lucky organisation—a good digestion, a healthy frame, a devil-may-care disposition."

"I wish I could make a similar boast," said Allan with a sigh.

"What do you sigh for? I hate a fellow that indulges in 'windy suspiration of forced breath,' even though he may be thinking of the beautiful Signora. But harkye, my fine fellow, my would-be *cavaliere servente*—you may be the Signora's fancy-man, and she may like you for blushing and playing mumchance, and so forth; but if you think to obtain any further favours you'll find yourself catawampously stumped, as the Yankees say. For correctness and character and all that sort of thing, she's a trump-card, and no mistake—a perfect Diana—(no, that won't do, I forgot Endymion, and half a dozen others)—quite a Lucretia or Virginia."

"Do you then imagine it possible," asked Allan rather indignantly "that I could be base enough to dream, even for a single moment——"

"Nay, nay, don't flare up, my touchy Congreve rocket! I imagine nothing, except that it is a friendly act to put you on your guard, to give you a *carte du pays,* as you confess that you're rather a Johnny Raw in London. Why, the Duke of Keswick offered her *carte blanche,* settlement, house, carriage, jewels, everything, and a precious shindy she kicked up; made old Antonio bundle him out of the house neck and crop. Then there's that old foxy humbug Lord Holloway always following her on the sly, and making her fine presents; and that drawling dandy fool young Cavendish, thinking to make sure of his Danaë because he can visit her in a shower of gold. She'll take the sparklers and the tin, for everything is fish that comes to her net; but as to the flats, they'll find themselves done, done as brown as the toast that was made of Tom Brown's brown bread, or my name isn't Harry Freeman: that's my vardict, and therefore I says it."

Thus chatting together they crossed Hyde Park, Freeman, who seemed to know everybody and everything, acting as cicerone, and finally conducting Allan to Tattersall's, as it was settling-day for an extra race that had been got up by some amateurs of the turf. Here the free-and-easy Harry appeared to be quite at home, nodding with the same good-humoured smile and familiar "How are you?" to a duke or a jockey. While he was engaged in conversation with a little knot of friends, Allan's attention was caught by a soft voice whose peculiarly winning accents were familiar to his ear, though he could not immediately recall where he had heard them, nor did his memory serve him when he took a leisurely survey of the speaker, a rather light-built, but compact and well-formed man, fashionably dressed, and courteous in his demeanour. A sudden turn of the head, however, having revealed to him a portion of a scar, imperfectly concealed by the whiskers, he recognised instantly the fellow-passenger of the stagecoach, whom he had so strongly suspected of being identical with the mysterious monk, and who had now added a pair of mustachios to his face. Delighted with this discovery, and impatient to gratify his curiosity, he was about to make application to his friend, when the stranger, lounging up to the spot where he was standing, exclaimed with a bland look and voice, "Good morning, Freeman." Without uttering a syllable, or in any way recognising the salutation, the party thus addressed fixed his eyes steadily upon the speaker, with an expression of indignant wonder that occasioned him to wheel lazily round, and saunter to another quarter, humming an air with a well-acted nonchalance as he retreated.

"Curse that fellow's impudence!" exclaimed Freeman; "to think of his addressing me—and at Tattersall's too!"

"Who is he—what is he?" eagerly asked Allan.

"He calls himself Captain Harcourt, but how he came by his commission or his aristocratic name, unless he purloined them, I really cannot tell you. I rather suspect that the Captain occasionally indulges in an alias. I can only tell you what *I* call him—namely—a scamp, a blackleg, a clever swindler, who knows just enough of the law to keep tolerably clear of its clutches, though he has been kicked off a racecourse more than once as a common cheat, and out of gaming-houses as a notorious rook and raff. I have heard that he formerly travelled to fairs with a gambling-booth of his own—I myself have only seen him when he has been enacting the man of fashion at races, prizefights, and public entertainments."

"But how came you acquainted with such a character?"

"By not knowing it—the fellow's manners are so plausible and even insinuating, his appearance so gentlemanly, his voice so winning, that I suffered him to cheat me at Newmarket in the sale of a spavined horse, a regular screw, on the strength of which he claimed my acquaintance; but as soon as I twigged that he was a flashman—one of the swell mob, I mizzled—gave him the cut direct. Spite of his wheedling ways the cove has lots of brass, but I never thought he would have come it so strong as to show his mug at Tattersall's; still less that he would venture upon such a saucy start as to tip me a 'Good morning, Freeman' "

Allan related the story of the stranger who had intruded himself into Chubbs's market-cart, and his reasons for suspecting that this Captain Harcourt was the same person as the apparent monk. "I should have thought it much more probable that he would have stolen a valuable gold watch, than have left it behind him," said Freeman. "No—no—you're on the wrong sniff there. The Captain's not such a flat, depend on't, as to drop his swag into a bunch of turnips. But enough of him and his dirty tricks. Faugh! I want an ounce of civet to sweeten my imagination, and so, as we stroll back towards the Opera House, I will talk to you of nothing but your fascinating friend, ay, and mine too, the beautiful Isola. How beautifully she sang that cavatina t' other night out of the Tancredi—and that charming aria out of the second act, the *'Giusto Ciel, che umile adoro!'* Hang me if she isn't a regular bang-up angel, and that's just the long and the short of the matter, and so—come on, Macduff!"

CHAPTER VII.

ALLAN had not yet been to the Opera, an entertainment of which he had heard so much, and had anticipated so great a treat from visiting it, that even a morning sight of the interior of the building, accompanied by Isola, presented itself to his imagination with a deep and undefinable sort of interest. A morning rehearsal, and a first rehearsal too, is perhaps the least attractive point of view in which any theatre or any performers can be contemplated, and it need excite little wonder, therefore, that Allan's earliest operatic impressions were those of grievous disappointment. After passing through a low and long passage, partially illumined by a few straggling lamps, and following his conductor through side-scenes rudely daubed over with figures, trees, and buildings, which the doubtful light would not allow him to discriminate, he emerged upon the stage, and gazed out upon a dim mysterious-looking hall, which wore the appearance of a vast subterranean cave or sepulchre.

The glimmering glass of the unlighted lustres deepened rather than dispersed the gloom; occasional voices of workmen or others, issuing from unseen recesses, echoed through the empty dome with an indistinct and unearthly sound; the vacant boxes, with their covered cushions and reversed draperies, looked dismal as the unoccupied cells of a catacomb; while the figures who had seated themselves in two or three parts of the lower tier, wore a strange and spectral aspect. Some of the band were in the orchestra, and, as the stage-lamps were partially lighted, Allan was enabled to discern more accurately the objects that surrounded him, which were not of a nature to obliterate his first feeling of disappointment. Everything appeared so dirty, coarse, and tawdry, that he could hardly believe himself to be in the London Opera House, of whose surpassing magnificence and refined taste he had heard and read such glowing accounts.

He gazed upwards, and saw suspended from the ceiling, threatening destruction to all below if their sustaining ropes should break, rocks, woods, and mountains, triumphal cars, fragments of carpentry, grinning monsters, altars, temples, gods and goddesses of different mythologies, all hanging together in complicated, but peaceful confusion. Nor was the scene below, as the performers successively arrived, a whit more consistent. Norma, which had not previously been acted by the present company, was the opera to be rehearsed. After many a note of preparation, and sundry curses from the stage-manager, coupled with repeated shouting of names, and threats of fining the absentees, the Gallic army, represented by six workmen bustling in all the martial panoply of paper caps, shirt-sleeves, and dirty brown-holland aprons, marched across the stage, when the chief priest of the Druids, dressed in a mackintosh coat, a bandana handkerchief, and splashed boots, took a pinch of snuff, removed the cigar from his mouth, and commenced the rehearsal by chanting a summons to the subordinate priests, who, in full chorus, called upon the moon to be quick in rising, which reminded the stage-manager to call out, "Jem Hopkins! see that the new lamp for the full moon is got ready, and tell Smithers to mend the thunder—the box is broken."

The Proconsul of the Romans, a celebrated warrior, next walked upon the stage, and taking off his clogs, his gloves, and his spencer, and folding up his umbrella, expressed a hope that he had not caught cold, as he had wetted his foot in running away from a dog, an animal of which he had always felt a peculiar dread;—after which he marched up to the foot-lamps without flinching, and sang as if he bade an equal defiance to catarrhs and catastrophes. Meanwhile the vestal priestesses— several of whom were in an interesting situation that promised an addition to the company—were cracking nuts and jokes with the bards and priests, and indulging in fun and foolery on the subject of a pot of porter, which the sacred choir were discussing, until it was time to come forward and sing a hymn, during the performance of which they looked becomingly demure and devout Even Isola, with her elegant morning dress and Leghorn bonnet of the last new fashion, presented, to Allan's eye, a most anomalous appearance as Norma, the Druidess. Nor was he less disappointed by her performance on this occasion, for after making every allowance for the embarrassment natural to the assumption of a new character, he could not help thinking that her singing and her acting were equally spiritless and ineffective, and he left the house with a determination never again to give himself the trouble of witnessing a rehearsal.

Little had Allan Latimer suspected, while walking home from the dinner-party at the Lum's, that he had continued to engross the sole attention of those young ladies long after his own disappearance, and the departure of the Snaggs and Popkins visitants. Huddled together in one of the bed-rooms, and too eagerly engaged to think of undressing, they all conjointly chanted his praises, each wishing to make it appear that she had been honoured with his particular and exclusive preference. "I found him a most delightful companion at dinner," observed Priscilla; "so attentive! he passed the mustard-pot to me twice, merely because I happened to say that I wouldn't give a farthing for boiled beef without it. One thing was still more pointed. I had called three times for bread, but Sally and the boy were both too busy to attend to me, when he said, with a tender look that I shall never forget, 'I have enough for both, and I shall be most happy if you will share my portion with me!'"

"And what of that?" sneered the jealous Amelia; "he couldn't do less. I suppose you thought it was a declaration of love."

"Depend upon it she considers it a regular pop. Hadn't you better speak to Pa, dear 'Cilla?" asked Harriet with a horse-laugh.

"Don't *you* talk, bo' son," retorted the elder sister; "flouncing down into the chair as you did, quite close to him, and throwing yourself into such an attitude."

"So she did," echoed Amelia; "and flirting with him at the tea-table too, when he evidently wanted to talk to me. However, I didn't care, for I had enough to do to attend to Nic Popkins, whose devoirs were very marked."

"And I'm sure *I* needn't care," resumed Priscilla, "for after he left us I went down to the parlour and found the toothpick which Mr. Latimer had dropped at dinner."

"La, 'Cilla! do you mean to use it?" inquired Amelia.

"I shouldn't mind it, for I never saw anything so clean and beautiful as his teeth; but I shall return it, of course. Ma and I can call for the purpose. It would be dreadfully shabby to keep it."

"Oh, my! How honest you've become all of a sudden!" sneered Amelia.

"And why of a sudden, Miss Wasp? Wasn't I always so?" Again the conversation reverted to Allan's figure, dress, deportment, and conversation—a subject so inexhaustible, that the clock struck twelve while they were yet discussing it.

"Lauk!" exclaimed Harriet, "I do declare it's midnight! Not that I care, for I don't believe in ghosts; but *did* you read that account in the 'Morning Post' of the apparition that appeared at Gravesend? That *must* be true, for it was all in black and white. There were three old ladies sitting together, as we may be now,—only we're young, you know; it was Sunday night, and one of them was reading aloud a poem called the 'Devil's Walk', when, just as they had finished"——At this moment a simultaneous scream burst from the three sisters, for the door opened, and a spectral-looking figure stalked slowly into the room. Their terrors, however, were allayed almost as soon as excited, for the apparition was presently discovered to be no other than Jemima, who, having just awoke, and hearing their voices, walked into the chamber in her night-gear, to inquire the cause of so late a conference. All three now fell foul of the poor spectre for frightening them, and in the midst of their wrangling, "Druidicus," putting his gaunt night-capped head out of his bed-room door, called up the stairs—"Girls! how dare you be making such a disturbance?— what *is* the matter?"

"Nothing," replied Amelia: "Jemima happened to frighten us sadly, that's all; but we are going to bed immediately."

"And what on earth has kept you up so late? Surely you have not got the last number of the magazine up stairs?"

"Yes we have, Pa!" replied the sly Amelia, winking at her sisters; "and we have been reading aloud your charming paper on the mistletoe."

"Well, well, go to bed directly, now that you have finished it. I cannot and will not allow such late hours. It is fortunate you didn't awake your mother."

Although Jemima returned on the following morning to her ringlets and her romance, she neither recovered her spirits nor her temper, for she had deemed herself most grievously ill-used in the whole affair of the dinner-party. If her sisters, however, had seen more of Allan Latimer at the time, she comforted herself with the reflection that she might think more of him afterwards. As it is well known that the thoughts of heroines are privileged to arrange themselves into spontaneous and unpremeditated stanzas of the most elaborate construction, it is little marvel that Jemima's pencil, which had been accustomed to draw patterns for embroidered collars, should quite unconsciously sketch a likeness of the object uppermost in her thoughts, whenever a piece of blank paper was placed beneath her fingers. A smile of peculiar satisfaction at her own performance having excited one morning the suspicion of Amelia, she crept on tiptoe to the table, and suddenly exclaimed—"Oh, 'Cilla! Oh, Harriet! here's fun! here's a discovery! Jemy has been attempting to draw a head of Mr. Latimer!"

"That I haven't!" cried the blushing delinquent, hastily adding an animal's body to the neck, and clapping four legs to the body;—"I was trying to draw a cow."

"Then I can only say," cried Priscilla, "that the cow is guilty of a base plagiarism in combing back the hair upon its forehead, and tying its cravat so exactly like Allan Latimer's." The sisterly burst of laughter that followed this sally so provoked the fair culprit, that she pettishly tore her drawing into little bits, which she threw into the faces of her accusers.

Deprived of this solace, poor Jemima became more moping and lackadaisical than ever, and as her mother knew her to be rather a weak-minded girl, who gave way to all sorts of nonsensical romance when not occupied, she was glad to employ her in making an inventory of the furniture, books, and effects of a handsome house in Russell Square, which had been placed in Mr. Lum's hands for sale.

High and unbounded as was the favour now enjoyed by Allan Latimer in this family, he was doomed—so uncertain, alas! are all sublunary honours and distinctions—not only to lose their good opinion still more rapidly than he had attained it, but o be looked on as a monster of duplicity by the very parties who had so recently been crying him up to the skies and contending for his smiles. Some friend having presented tickets to Miss Lum and her brother, they went to a public concert at which Signora Guardia was to sing, and there, to their utter consternation and amazement, they beheld Allan Latimer, the son of the lady who kept a carriage, and the heir of the rich old merchant, doing duty as one of the band. Having ascertained that their eyes had not deceived them, they concluded that his appearance might have been a freak, he might be only performing as an amateur; but on application to one of the clarionet players, with whom Tom was slightly acquainted, he was apprised that the delinquent attended in a professional capacity, that he was paid for his exertions, and moreover that he was a regular teacher of the violoncello. Misfortunes never come singly. The next morning's post brought a letter to "Druidicus," who had written to an acquaintance at Woodcote on the subject of Allan, informing him that he had wantonly quarrelled with the rich old merchant, who had dismissed and disowned him, and that he had clandestinely run away from home, after having behaved in a very scandalous way to a charming girl, whose affections he had won under the pretext of an honourable courtship. And that such a wretch should dare to intrude himself into such a respectable family as the Lums! and evidently with the same intentions too, for each of the four sisters claimed him as a decided, though not a declared suitor. It was the very acme of enormity. A false hearted runaway!—a pauper!—a fiddler! was successively ejaculated by three of the sisters; but the tender-hearted Jemima rather objected to the latter word as a term of reproach, observing with a sigh—"How beautiful that white hand must look when performing! And if he does play upon the fiddle, it's not a common one; you said yourself, dear 'Cilla, that it was a very large one!"

"Tom!" exclaimed Harriet, whose boatswain's spirit was aroused, "you ought to fight the fellow."

"Well, and I shouldn't mind it"—replied the brother—"if I were to put myself in training for a month under Joe Simmons."

"Why, you don't think I mean fisticuffs, do you? No, you ought to hire a pistol, and challenge him."

"Oh! my service to you: I know a trick worth two of that. Those scamps are always good shots, and I've no fancy whatever for a bullet in the thorax."

"It was a fraudulent act, my dear Mrs. L.," sighed "Druidicus," who had just been paying last week's bills, "to put us to the expense of that dinner; nay, I may say a swindling act, for it was obtaining another man's goods under false pretences; but our most proper course is to take no notice of him unless he should call, in which case I shall know how to dismiss him with a becoming dignity. I will let him see that a distinguished writer in the Antiquarian Magazine is not a person to be insulted with impunity."

A few days after this colloquy Allan Latimer, little dreaming of the reception that awaited him, presented himself in Great Russell Street, when Tom, thinking he might be called on to assist in a forcible ejectment, happened to recollect that he had an appointment with Nic Popkins, and ran off to the Museum, as if in great apprehension of being too late. Mrs. Lum kept purposely out of the way, assigning as a reason—"that it was a subjick she didn't ought to interfere in;—that it made the blood bile in her veins; and she feared, if she saw him, she might give him sich a blowing-up as would derange her stomach, for she was always indigestible when she got into a passion." Allan was, therefore, consigned to the father alone, while two of the girls listened at the drawing-room door, and two others looked over the banisters from above to watch his exit. After the complainant had pompously delivered himself of a long speech, which he had learnt by heart for the occasion, Allan, all amazement at the charges brought against him without even a shadow of foundation, would have entered on his defence; but as the indignant "Druidicus" not only refused to hear him, but bade him quit the house, and never darken his doors again, he made his bow, and left the apartment hastily dispersing the listeners in his exit, and saluted, as he reached the passage below, by a quadruple hiss from the upper floor.

Allan would have felt indignant at this unceremonious dismissal, had not the charges brought against him appeared so truly absurd and preposterous that they rather provoked contempt and laughter than any enduring wrath. In losing the society of such a family there was little to regret, but he was annoyed at having incurred even their unmerited enmity, and was therefore doubly gratified when he was shortly furnished with an opportunity of returning good for evil by rendering them an essential service.

It has been stated that Jemima had been deputed to take an inventory of all the goods, chattels, plate, books, and other effects of a handsome house in Russell Square, during the intervals of which occupation she amused herself by an occasional stroll in the enclosure of the square, feeding her imagination with the pastoral images suggested by the brown grass and forlorn-looking trees, and only regretting that she could conjure up no shepherd to recreate her with his pipe—no knight, cavalier, or other hero to whisper tales of love, or to bear her off upon his palfrey to the rose-encircled altar of Hymen. What, then, was her delight, while plunged in one of these reveries, to behold a figure approaching whose frogged and tasselled military coat, whose whiskered and mustachoed cheek, whose graceful walk, and whose distinguished air proclaimed at once the soldier and the gentleman! After looking at him through her ringlets as he passed, she cast her eyes demurely upon the ground, walked on, turned round when she reached the boundary of the enclosure, and finding, as the stranger had done exactly the same, that they were again about to meet, she called up the prettiest look of confusion and embarrassment which could possibly be summoned at so very short a notice. It may well be imagined that this becoming agitation was not diminished when the stranger, politely bowing, exclaimed in a voice and manner of the most winning suavity—"I beg your pardon for the liberty I am taking, but will you allow me to remind you that the grass is damp, and that, if you wear thin shoes, you may be running some risk of catching cold."

"Thank you, Sir; but I always wear double-soled shoes, and I never catch cold," was the rather unromantic reply. Her companion was delighted to hear it, and again, in deprecating strains, implored her forgiveness for having presumed to address her. Nor were his supplications vain, for Jemima, immeasurably delighted at finding herself thus tête-à-tête *with a* bonâ fide mustachoed officer, became every moment less and less disposed to be inexorable, as she discovered that his eyes were soft and gentle as his voice, his manners insinuating, his discourse that of a remarkably clever man, for he talked of nothing but her beauty, her ringlets, and his own good fortune in having accidentally encountered so charming, so fascinating a person. With that frankness which is so characteristic of a soldier, he then informed her that he was a Captain in the army, a man of high family, that he had served in General Evans's Legion in Spain, where he had received a wound, and that being a single man and in independent circumstances, he had some thought of travelling for a few months, though he might perhaps be induced, after all, to settle permanently in England. As such a spontaneous confidence justified a little curiosity in return, he put a few questions to Jemima, who, not thinking it necessary to make any admissions that might tend to terminate an acquaintance so auspiciously commenced and so exceedingly desirable, contented herself with stating that she resided in the Square, pointing at the same time to the handsomest house it contained. After a long and rather a tender colloquy, considering it was a first one, she took her leave, having previously mentioned, by mere chance, that she was accustomed to walk in the enclosure every day at the same hour, Observing that the stranger watched her to the door, she gave a consequential knock, as if she was the proprietor of the mansion, swept in with a dignified air, hurried up stairs, and threw herself upon a sofa, in a state of fluttering and joyous excitement such as she had never before experienced.

Possessing much of that cunning which is often the most strongly developed in the weakest-minded people, rendered flighty by the romances she had read, and justifying herself by the dictum that in love and war all stratagems are fair, Jemima now began a course of deception which a wiser head might have been puzzled either to devise or to execute with equal ingenuity and success. In their subsequent interviews at the same place of rendezvous she represented herself as an orphan living with her uncle, who was at present in Gloucestershire, looking after her estate, and preparing "the Hall" for her reception, as she would shortly attain the age of twenty-one, and meant thenceforward to reside in the country.

"You said *the Hall,*" whispered the Captain in a tone of tender inquiry. "Is it your own? and is it, like yourself, handsome?"

"It is my own," replied Jemima demurely, as if she wished to disclaim all merit on that account—"and it certainly is rather a fine place. Built in the Elizabethan style—(her memory and the last romance here supplied her with a ready-made mansion, which she determined to build on a handsome scale, since it was to cost her nothing,)—with embattled coping, a tower at one corner surmounted by a crocketed spire, and projecting casemented windows, its quadrangular form imparts to it a rather heavy appearance, which, however, is amply compensated by the capaciousness, I might almost say the grandeur, of its interior arrangements. Lofty and antique, the Hall opens upon a terrace decorated with statues and shaded at each extremity by a lofty cypress, whence a flight of marble steps leads to the gardens, laid out in the formal style of Louis the Fourteenth. I am well aware that this style has its admirers, but I am free to confess that I myself prefer a more simple and natural character in gardening; and as to those gloomy old cypresses, I am determined, as soon as I am mistress of the place, to have them cut down."

"Doubtless," observed the Captain with an air of perfect unconcern—"there are lands attached to the Hall, which bring in a handsome revenue."

"Not above two or three thousand a year at present, but my uncle says the farms are underlet, and he means to see about raising the rents, in which I hope he will succeed, for I have no other property except the house in Russell Square." This ingenious declaration was unnecessary; she had said quite enough. As the Captain happened at that moment to be labouring under a severe attack of impecuniosity, and had consequently no time to lose, he made love to his fair innamorata at full gallop, and as the heroine of the ringlets and romance had nearly completed her inventory of the house, and would only have a few days left for the completion of the adventure, she was in as great a hurry to accept, as the Captain was to offer his hand.

Eager and impassioned as he pretended to be, and penniless as he really was, a latent misgiving haunted the mind of the lover, who, finding it difficult to believe that so great an heiress, and so great a simpleton, should be thus thrown, unsought, into his arms, intimated a wish to be introduced to the aunt, which would enable him, he thought, to judge for himself. This was a startling proposition, but as Jemima was not going to lose a mustachoed man of family and fortune almost as soon as she had found him, her cunning, quickened by her wishes, soon enabled her to surmount the difficulty. The house being in the charge of an old man and his wife, who were easily prevailed upon by a small gratuity to become her confederates, she took from the wardrobe of the deceased lady to whom it had belonged, a handsome dress with appropriate ornaments, in which she arrayed the dame, while the husband, tricked out for the nonce in a showy livery, did duty as porter. All the other servants were stated to be at the Hall, preparing it for her reception.

These preliminaries being arranged, the Captain was introduced into the house, which he found expensively furnished and appointed; and to the pretended aunt, who supported her own character and that of her niece with a due dignity. Jemima, she observed, was not only an heiress, but a very sweet girl, and it was not to be supposed that her uncle, whose return was daily expected, would suffer her to bestow her hand upon any one whose character and circumstances would not bear the strictest investigation. Though the Captain's doubts were now dispelled, his fears of the uncle were increased, especially when Jemima despondingly admitted that he was very particular and very cross.

"Why, then," demanded the suitor, "should we not fly at once from tyranny and wretchedness, to liberty and love? The railroad will speed us towards Gretna Green, and when we are once united, we may defy uncles, fate, and fortune, and devote the remainder of our lives to happiness unalloyed." Jemima, concealing with the greatest difficulty her unbounded delight at the success of her manœuvres, affected to give an unwilling consent. The following morning was appointed for their flight, and the Captain handed her from a hackney-coach to the railroad-station precisely at the moment when Allan Latimer reached the same spot, in one of his promenades to visit the different lions of the metropolis. "Miss Jemima with Captain Harcourt!" he exclaimed, gazing with astonishment at the latter, upon whose arm she was familiarly leaning: "Will you allow me to inquire whether you are acquainted with this person?"

"Yes, Sir," replied the damsel pertly; "and I know him to be a true-hearted man and a gentleman, and not a breaker of his vows, as you are."

"I very much doubt it. Let me implore you to be on your guard, for I have reason to believe that your companion is no better than he should be—in fact, that he is an adventurer and a sharper."

"Damnation, Sir!" ejaculated the Captain, darting an eat-him-up-alive look at Allan—"do you mean to apply these terms to me?"

"I do, Captain Harcourt!" was the reply; "and I beg to add, that I am not to be bullied either by big words or angry looks. If I have been misinformed, I shall be happy to recall them. In the mean time there is my card, if you wish to know who it is that claims the right to advise, and, if necessary, to protect this lady."

"But she has placed herself under my protection, and you will interfere between us at your peril."

"I shall do so, nevertheless, until I have ascertained that her present proceeding is sanctioned by her parents."

"Parents, Sir!—she has none: she is an orphan and an only child."

"What strange delusion is this? She is the daughter of Mr. Jonas Lum, a respectable house-agent in Great Russell Street, and has a mother living, besides a brother and three sisters."

"House-agent! house-agent!" muttered the Captain, letting go the arm of his companion, as his thoughts reverted to the mansion in Russell Square "Jemima! dearest Jemima! you hear what this audacious man says: can it be possible that you belong to that horrid family in Great Russell Street?"

"I must confess," sighed Jemima, blushing crimson, as she saw that her detection was inevitable, "that I *have* rather got a father there."

"And in some little degree, perhaps, a mother, and brother, and sisters!" sneered her lover. Her confused silence and downcast looks gave consent to the charge. "But the Hall—the estate in Gloucestershire—is not *that* yours?"

"Not quite—not altogether," stammered the embarrassed girl—"I must confess that—of the two—I have rather not got any estate anywhere; but what signify riches or estates?—when two fond hearts like ours—"

"Oh, Gammon!" interposed the Captain fiercely—"none of your blarney! Here's a precious rig! Who would ever have thought that I should be so regularly hocussed by such a poodle-headed kid! There's nothing left for it but to cut my stick!" With these words he spun round upon his heel, and diving among the carriages and carts collected at the station, was out of sight in a twinkling.

"And I sha'n't run away to Gretna Green, and I sha'n't have a mustachoed husband after all," cried Jemima, bursting into tears.

By communicating to her what he had learnt respecting the pretended Captain, and assuring her that she ought to be most grateful to Heaven for her escape, Allan partially succeeded in calming the deserted damsel, who was now only apprehensive that her flight might be discovered by the family.

"If you are quick in your movements," said Allan, "that may yet be prevented. The hackney-coach has not yet been discharged; return in it immediately, and let me beseech you to take warning from the great peril you have escaped, and not suffer yourself to be again cajoled by an adventurer and a scamp." Without confessing how much of the cajolery, upon the present occasion, was imputable to herself, the forlorn damsel thanked him for his timely interference, reseated herself in the hackney-coach, and wept all the way as she was driven back in "maiden meditation"—but by no means "fancy free"—to the completion of her inventory in Russell Square.

CHAPTER VIII.

"MON Doo!" exclaimed Mrs. Glossop, lifting up her hands and eyes as the poor wounded lunatic was slowly and carefully helped out of the carriage at the door of the Manor-House—"here's a *coup de grace*—here's a *misericorde* business. Why, the poor creature's covered with blood—her teeth are chattering in her head, her clothes are all wringing wet, and she has neither a bonnet nor a shawl: it's enough to give her a perfect *malapropos.*"

"Come, come," cried Brown peevishly, "don't stand there *parlez-vousing,* but bustle about and have a good fire in the yellow room, and get her to bed as fast as you can, and make some of that famous posset immediately. The poor creature is out of her wits, and, I fear, may have fallen into the river, or met with some accident."

"Pauvre garçon!—Only to think. Dear, dear! we have not a moment to lose, for she doesn't seem to *portez vous bien* by any means. Here, Susan! Susan!—tell cook to boil some milk immediately."

"Where's John? where's Trotman?" demanded Brown, pacing up and down the room in a state of great perplexity.

"I saw him this moment running full speed out of the grounds towards the Green."

"Ah! always the same—always out of the way when he's wanted. Did he say where he was going?"

"Not he—when does he ever say anything?"

"Never—except in monosyllables—speaks like a popgun, one pellet at a time.

Well—what are you waiting for? I told you to be quick."

"Yes, Sir, but you stopped me just as I was going. Here, Susan, cook, Susan!"

The lunatic meanwhile, who had been placed in the *fauteuil,* with her wounded arms supported by those of the chair, preserved unbroken the silence which she had maintained in the carriage; but, although she made no complaint, she seemed to be suffering severely from the effects of wet and cold, her whole frame shaking violently, her teeth chattering, and her eyes rolling from side to side with great wildness and rapidity. "Going into a rampant raging fit," muttered Brown, half afraid of being overheard—"See it—know it—feel it—fly at me presently, like a wild cat—hear her sharpening her teeth on purpose—scratch my eyes out in no time—make a salad-bowl of the sockets—fill them up with pepper, mustard, vinegar—perhaps a red-hot coal—maniacs are never particular—no use resisting—strong as twenty men—no doubt she could turn me inside out, like skinning a rabbit, if she tried. No Bedlam neither in the country, where they want it twice as much, for people must be mad indeed to live in it. And that rascal Trotman to run away at the very moment when I wanted to send him for Dawson the apothecary.

Really that fellow's inattention and thought lessness are quite——"

A moan from the suffered and a slight movement of the chair, converted the completion of the sentence into an exclamation of "Zounds! she's getting her steam up—going to explode—about to make a spring at me!"

Brave as he was under ordinary circumstances. Brown was not free from superstition; and a maniac appeared in his eyes so nearly allied to something supernatural, especially when in a raging state, that he flew to the bell, and continued ringing it with the vigour of great nervous excitement. Mrs. Glossop and two maids soon hastened into the room, the former provided with a warm shawl, which she placed lightly over the strange lady, when she inquired whether they should assist her up stairs, as the bed-room was ready. Their master signified assent, and, to his great comfort, the lunatic, instead of offering any resistance, exhibited a perfect docility, and even seemed thankful for the feeling and considerate way in which they supported her towards the door.

Emboldened by this tranquil demeanour, and anxious to throw off all suspicion of fear from himself, by imputing it, right or wrong, to others, he exclaimed, almost contemptuously, "Don't be frightened, Mrs. Glossop: Susan, what the deuce makes you look so pale?—why, Mary! you seem to tremble. What cowards you all are! The unfortunate lady is as quiet as a lamb.—I have just been travelling with her for miles, and if it hadn't been for her moaning and crying all the way, I should have thought her a very pleasant companion. There—gently! don't touch her arms— slowly up the stairs. Take care of her, Mrs. Glossop, and don't forget the posset."

"An ugly job this," continued the merchant, not sorry to find himself once more alone. "What on earth am I to do with a mad lady in the house? can't manage women when they're in their senses—never could—never tried, that's one good thing. Ha, ha! that's a wipe for the whole sex. Pretty affair if I can't get rid of her— made keeper of a rural bedlam—stick up a board—'Manor-House mad-house,—by Adam Brown.—N.B. Handcuffs and strait-waistcoats to be sold, on the most reasonable terms, with an allowance to those who take a quantity.' "

While soliloquising in this half-angry, half-burlesque strain, the door opened, and John Trotman, covered with perspiration and almost breathless from the haste with which he had been running, panted out the words, "Want me, Sir?"

"Yes, sirrah, and so I have for the last half-hour. What the devil do you mean by running out of the way at such a time as this—at the very moment when I wanted to send you for Mr. Dawson, the apothecary?"

"Been there—seen him—coming directly," was the reply.

"Why, you don't mean to say that you have been all the way to the Green and back in this time?" The servant nodded.

"And who sent you?"

"Nobody—saw the lady was ill—no time to lose—couldn't wait."

"John! you're not such a fool as I thought, and I'm a greater one than I thought."—A respectful bow signified assent to both propositions, when the taciturn Trotman, not wishing, as it would seem, to remain any longer with his self-stultified master, walked panting out of the room.

The apothecary, who soon found his way to the house, gave its owner reason to fear that some time would elapse before he could be got out of it again; for he intimated that, without any reference to the mental malady, upon which he would not for the present venture to give an opinion, he apprehended a tedious if not a serious illness from the exposure to wet and cold, which had struck a perilous chill to the whole system of the patient. Trotman's hasty application being removed, proper bandages were substituted for the wounds in the arm, which were unimportant; a composing-draught and other remedies were administered; every arrangement was made that might contribute to her comfort; one of the maids was directed to sit up with her; the patient, who appeared to be exhausted by previous fatigue and excite-ment, slept soundly during the remainder of the night, and awoke on the following morning in a much more tranquil though equally dementated state.

An adventure of any sort is so rare a godsend in a quiet and secluded district, that the village of Woodcote might deem itself singularly fortunate in being sup-plied with a new and still more startling mystery before that of the Monk had received the smallest elucidation or lost any of its interest. Incessant were the in-quiries, conjectures, and gossipings elicited by this strange occurrence; long and frequent were the consultations friends summoned by Brown to aid him with their counsel, or attracted by their own curiosity, either to obtain a peep at the lunatic, or to pick up some additional topics for tittle-tattle and surmise. Apprehending that the invalid might have escaped from some madhouse, or private receptacle for such patients, it was Brown's first care to insert advertisements in all the county and local newspapers, describing the dress and personal appearance of the unhappy stranger, the circumstances under which she was first discovered, and the place where she might now be found; but although these notices were frequently repeated, and ev-ery other means resorted to that seemed likely to afford a clue to her history, every perquisition failed, no letter upon the subject. was received from any quarter, no applicant appeared.

The object of all this solicitude and curiosity excited the deepest interest in those who had the most frequent opportunities of observing her, for as Dawson's prognostications were fortunately not verified, her bodily health not having under-gone any permanent derangement, she was now allowed to walk about the house, always accompanied, however, by one of the maids. Not only was she perfectly quiet and harmless, but she seemed every day to acquire an additional composure; and, though her faculties remained in the same alienated state, she would occasion-ally pore over a book with an evident comprehension of its import, and had been observed to listen to the music of an itinerant band with great apparent pleasure. Only for very short periods, however, could any object or pursuit retain her atten-tion, her thoughts soon relapsed into abstraction or vacancy, her eyes never lost their wild and wandering expression.

Unwilling to trust implicitly to the opinion of the village apothecary, Brown summoned from Cheltenham an eminent practitioner who had paid particular attention to cases of lunacy, engaging him to remain for two or three days at the Manor-House, that he might be the better qualified to form a correct judgment upon the case. It was the deliberate opinion of this gentleman that the patient was not afflicted with hereditary or organic insanity, but that her derangement was the probable result of some violent shock to the nervous system, the effect of which might either be worn out by time, or be abruptly removed by some other vehement and unexpected excitement, of which latter mode of cure, strange as it might appear, he had known several instances.

Kind and gentle treatment was recommended, with every indulgence calculated to soothe, occupy, or amuse the mind; but as there was reason to apprehend that she had recently been subjected to accesses of violent delirium, which might possibly recur, he desired that she might be always accompanied or kept in sight by some attendant, who should avoid all appearance of restraining her actions, or even of suspecting her sanity. Upon the probable duration of her malady he would not offer an opinion.

"Better and better!" exclaimed Brown, as he feed and dismissed the son of Esculapius. "Nobody can find out who she is or what she is; the doctor can't tell when she is likely to recover, which may be never, and in the mean time here am I to have the pleasure of maintaining a mad lady in my house, with a maid or keeper to dance attendance at her heels, and some fine moonlight night, as a return for all my kindness,

I may have the pleasure of finding that my grateful patient has burnt my house about my ears, or cut my throat with my own carving-knife."

"My good friend," replied Roger Crab, to whom this Jeremiade was addressed, "it is doubtless an unfortunate affair in every point of view—but in these cases, whatever may be the customs of society, the claims of humanity are paramount. Thank God! I know nothing of law; but even if you are not legally bound to maintain this poor lady, I maintain that you ought to be."

"Pleasant, but wrong! How can you make that out?"

"Listen, and I will tell you. What a fuss and turmoil have lords of the manor and others made about their right to strays and waifs, and *flotson* and *jetson,* whenever there was anything to be gained by them! No want of eager claimants in *that* case. Well, here is a stray and a waif, which, instead of bringing a profit, imposes a trouble and expense—and you are the lord of the manor. If you have a claim to make in one case, you have a duty to perform in the other. Had it been a treasure-trove, it would have been yours as the finder; it proves to be a treasure-trove reversed, and the loss, therefore, must be yours."

"Don't care a farthing about the expense—shall maintain her, and take care of her, till I discover her friends, and even if I don't; but what worries me is the bother, the trouble, the nuisance, the risk, the responsibility.—I wish I knew how a fellow might get rid of all that."

"Nothing in life so easy," cried Captain Molloy, who at this moment swaggered into the room, accompanied by Mrs. Latimer. "Send her to the poor-house, as a vagrant, whose parish can't be found: they will clap a strait waistcoat upon her, shut her up in the infirmary, and there she is, off your hands, as clean as a whistle."

"Heaven forbid! How can you talk so unfeelingly?" said Mrs. Latimer, departing for a moment from her usual placid smile and gentle voice. "I know Mr. Brown too well to believe him capable of such conduct. No doubt it must be very awkward and distressing to any gentleman to have such an inmate in his house; in fact, she ought to be in charge of some lady, and, if you would let her come to my cottage, there's Allan's bed, you know, and I'm sure I and dear Walter would do everything in our power to—— "

"No, no, my good lady," interposed Brown; "the tree shall lie where it has fallen, and no one shall have charge of her but myself, whatever may be the annoyance. You have most kindly done everything in your power already—been here early and late, and all day long. Have you supplied her with a present wardrobe, as I desired?"

"I have had her own clothes set to rights, and have added what may be immediately required."

"And what is your opinion," inquired Crab, "as to the probable position she may have held in society? Having seen so much more of her than anybody else, you are better qualified to form a judgment."

"That she is a lady I have never entertained a moment's doubt. Not only do her young face, delicate form, and features evince gentle birth, but her gracious and graceful though silent manner of acknowledging my little attentions proves to me that she has been accustomed to good society. Then her clothes were such as no person of inferior station would have worn, and there are costly pearl rings in her ears, to which she seems to attach value, as she loves to examine them before a glass."

"Did I not hear," inquired Crab, "that she had testified pleasure at the music of a passing band?"

"Yes; and as soon as dear Walter learnt it, he suggested that Ellen should bring her guitar, and there they have been playing and singing to her for more than an hour this morning, and I'm sure I shall never forget it. Ellen, to be sure, does play very sweetly, and nothing can be more touching than Walter's voice when he warbles a plaintive ballad; but to see how the poor lady sat listening with her eyes fixed, and her mouth half open, and her figure motion-less, as if her whole soul were in her ears! And when Ellen laid down the guitar the poor lady took it up, and played snatches of tunes with a very finished touch of her little white fingers, and sang broken fragments of songs in tones so wild, and so plaintive, and so startling, that it made my very heart ache to hear her. And then she seemed to be trying to recollect some tune, for she began and left off again several times, and looked up to the ceiling, and, finding she could not succeed, she put down the guitar, and shook her head mournfully, and burst into tears. I don't know when I have seen a. more distressing sight."

"Oh, then! it's Walter and my Ellen, when they're singing together, that would charm the heart out of your body, like a bird out of a bush," cried Molloy, who now seized every opportunity of puffing these parties in the presence of Adam Brown. "I can answer for my Ellen—kind-hearted creature!—doing everything in her power to comfort the poor mad lady; and as to Walter, there isn't a better fellow in the whole world! Somebody told me he talked of leaving us, and embarking in busi-ness. Bad luck to the thought of it! It will be a sad day for all of us when he leaves Wood-cote."

"That it will indeed, dear boy!" sighed the mother.

"And cannot you gather any information from the lady's discourse?" inquired Crab, reverting to the previous subject.

"No, indeed; for she rarely speaks at all, and never more than a very few words coherently. And yet she can read to herself for a short time, and evidently understands what she peruses, for I saw her smile at a French extract from one of Molière's plays—which is another proof that she is a person of education."

"Then there is yet a hope," resumed Crab, "from such glimmerings of intelligence, that with time, and care, and kindness, we may succeed in curing her malady; and, as friends and neighbours of Mr. Brown, I think we ought not to throw the whole trouble and annoyance upon his shoulders, but come freely forward, every one of us, and bear our share of the burthen. What say you, Mrs. Latimer?"

"I can answer for myself and Walter—nothing will give us greater pleasure; and with Mr. Brown's permission I will come up to the Manor-House regularly every day."

As a proposal for sharing the burthen sounded, in Molloy's ears, very like undertaking to divide the expense,—a process which, for various reasons, might prove exceedingly inconvenient to him,—he thought it necessary to put in a timely *caveat* by exclaiming, "By the powers! there isn't a more charitable man, though I say it that shouldn't say it, than Charles Sullivan Molloy—that is to say, in my own circle."

"Circle, indeed! for it ends where it begins—namely, at home," muttered Crab, abstractedly tapping the ends of his own fingers, as if he were engaged in some process of mental arithmetic. "This sort of round-robin munificence, this spherical generosity, is the most gratifying of all, for it costs nothing."

"I am obliged," pursued the Captain, "to refuse myself the pleasure of all such donations in England, for I consider the poor of Clognakilty and the County Down to have a prior claim upon me, and the gums I give away among them are unknown."

"*That* I believe," said Crab, with an air of very significant assent.

"In fact, I am obliged to do a great deal in my own neighbourhood, for——"

"Charity covereth a multitude of sins," interposed Crab; "though, in the Proverbs of Solomon, I believe the word is love, and not charity,—but I suppose they are synonymous."

"However, I don't complain, for we have good authority for saying that what we thus bestow will be returned to us seven-fold, even in this world."

"Ay, ay, Captain! ***Solas quas dederis semper habebis opes***—the only riches you always retain are those you have given away. No charitable man therefore can ever plead poverty."

"Faith, then! I'm not the man to do that, and no need; better luck for me! But one can't be lavishing in all directions. My expenses in that way at Clognakilty House are monstrous; quite incredible!"

"Perfectly!" ejaculated Crab.

"However, I am not the man, I say, to boast of my benevolence. What I give away among my own people in Ireland, in addition to my English claims, is neither here nor there." Crab nodded with judicial gravity, as much as to say, "The court is with you."

"I repeat that I don't want to make a brag of these things, nor do they concern others, for I am quite aware that my private charities are nothing to anybody."

"There I agree with you ***verbatim et literatim***" cried Crab. "Oh! how pleasant is it when neighbours agree together—in charity!"

"What's all this sparring and fencing about?" demanded Brown. "If any of you imagine that I shall suffer you to bear one farthing of the expense to which I may be put by this poor lunatic, you'll find yourselves deucedly mistaken. Not such a shabby fellow. What! think you've got to deal with a pauper? Flatter myself I have more than seven and ninepence in my pocket at ***present;***—rather think I'm in pretty good credit;—have a strong suspicion that the Manor-House estate belongs to me; that my account at the banker's is not overdrawn; and that my name is in the books of the Bank of England. Ha! ha!" His cane was rapped affirmatively upon the ground as he cast a challenging look at his auditors, which seemed to inquire whether any of them would dare to gainsay his assertions.

"Mrs. Glossop," said the merchant to his housekeeper, two or three days after the colloquy, "poor Susan chambermaid looks very pale, and I'm afraid she'll be knocked up presently if she's to be always dancing attendance upon our patient. Besides, we can't spare her, and I've been thinking we ought to engage somebody on purpose to wait upon the invalid, and toddle about the house and grounds with her, and watch her, for she may, perhaps, try to escape again, or get into some fresh mischief."

"I'm sure, Sir, I'm glad to hear you say so, for we can't never go in this dreadfully *a la bonne heure* way. It's quite one person's work to attend to her, but I s'pose it won't last long, and that you'll soon send her away *shay voo.*"

"No such luck! no such luck! for aught I know to the contrary, she may live and die here."

"*Mon doo,* Sir! you don't mean to say so. What, keep her here as long as she's a *bon vivant?* And such a nice, pretty, genteel young woman too. La, sir! what will the people say? What a scandal it will make! How all the gossips and neighbours will lift up their hands and eyes!"

"Mrs. Glossop! I think I told you some time ago that all the gossips and neighbours might go to the devil, and that you had my permission to follow them. That liberal offer I beg leave to repeat."

"La, Sir! how can you talk so? Whatever you wish must, of course, be done and I'm sure I've taken my share in attending to her."

"Now, I was thinking," pursued Brown, "of engaging Fanny Chubbs to come and stay with us as the poor lady's servant and companion. She's a nice girl, is Fanny, and I dare say she would like the change; and it might do her good, for she would live better here than she can at the farm, and she looks very peaky and delicate. Keep her supplied with the posset I ordered?"

"Yes, Sir; she has it once a-week, and sometimes twice; but still, as I told her mother, in my flagitious way, and though Fanny does her best to conceal it, it's evident to me that she's in a very bad way, in fact, quite a *malade imaginaire*"

"Well, then, I'll walk over to Four-oak Farm myself, and speak to Mrs. Chubbs on the subject. Nothing like time present, and what a fellow does himself is generally well done."

Most inauspicious and inopportune for the inmates of the farm was the moment selected for his visit, John Chubbs having just then been led home in a glorious state of intoxication, after celebrating, in company with Jem Belcher and two or three others, the anniversary of one of the battles in which he had been engaged. Being just in that happy medium between singing, hiccoughing, and approaching drowsiness, when the drunkard, imagining himself to be still sober, mistakes a blind doggedness for a proof of rationality and free will, he had seated himself upon a large linen-chest that stood near the fire, still holding in his mouth the pipe which had stimulated his deep potations, and obstinately resisting all his wife's entreaties that he would suffer himself to be helped up-stairs and put to bed. Throwing frequent and anxious glances at the window while she was thus occupied,—for she dreaded the approach of any visitant who might detect him in this disreputable state,—the good woman suddenly uttered a suppressed cry, followed by the terrified exclamation of, "O goodness gracious me! what *will* become of us all? Sure as ever I be a living woman, here's the Squire a coming, and if John is cotched in this here state we shall all be ruinated for good and all! Here, Fanny dear, bear a hand—quick—quick—let's see if we can't get him up-stairs." Weakened by her previous illness and present agitation, Fanny could render but little assistance. Chubbs, resisting their purpose, would not allow himself to be supported farther than to the next chair, into which he heavily sank, vainly trying to hiccough the burthen of a barrack song, and half unconsciously, but very firmly, clinging to the seat when they essayed to move him farther.

"Mother! mother!" cried Fanny, glancing at the window, "the Squire has got to the garden-gate. What *shall* we do? We can never move him; but can't we hide him in the chest? he'll fall asleep in a minute."

"So he will, so he will," replied the mother, at the same time pushing the chair to the side of the chest, and throwing open the lid. By their joint exertions the drunken man was rolled into the receptacle, falling upon the linen at the bottom without offering any further resistance, under the mistaken notion that his own bed and bedroom had been brought down-stairs, and placed near the fire, which he seemed to think a very great improvement upon the ordinary arrangement and construction of the house. The lid was closed; Fanny, not knowing in her confusion how to employ herself, flew to an empty churn, which she plied with as much energy as if she were working for her life; while the mother, still red and out of breath from her exertions, hurried to the door, and received her dreaded visitant with as many low curtsies as if she did not heartily wish him at York or Jericho.

Brown entered the room in a bad humour. He hated all people who ran in debt, more especially where the money was owing to himself, and a single survey with his keen suspicious eye presently assured him that his chance of payment had been diminished, rather than increased, since his last visit. On all sides he beheld evidence of an arduous and painful struggle between the cleanly industry of the wife and daughters, and the poverty forced upon the family by the intemperate habits of the master. The hams and farm produce which he had seen hanging from the beam on his previous visit had disappeared, as well as a portion of the furniture and the shining garniture of the huge mantel-shelf; several broken panes of glass were cleverly repaired with paper; and the dress of both mother and daughter, though still clean and neat, was patched and threadbare. Stern and inflexible as is the morality that is based upon principle, it is less inexorable than that which springs from interest; no wonder, therefore, that Brown's virtuous indignation against Chubbs's bibulous sins flared up the more strongly as he noticed these diminished probabilities of ever obtaining the overdue rent. Just as he was about to launch into an angry invective against sots, his eye fell upon Fanny, and, as the current of his thoughts changed, his mood softened into gentleness and ruth. "Fanny, dear," he exclaimed in an affectionate tone, "you still look very, very poorly. Does Mrs. Glossop send you the posset regularly?"

"Yes, Sir,—yes, thankye, Sir," was the curtsying and blushing reply; "and I am sure I don't know how I shall ever be grateful enough for all your kindness."

"Nor I either," echoed the mother.

"Well, then, I'll tell you what you shall do, so as to render a service both to yourself and me, to say nothing of the poor lady up at the Manor-House."—He then detailed his plan, and stated the wages he proposed to pay her; but as his financial faculty was always quickened, and his moral sense a little blunted, whenever he drove a bargain of any sort, he could not help adding that he should deduct the amount of her wages from the debt due by the father.

"O, Sir! I shall be so happy to accept your offer!" cried Fanny, clasping her hands together in the delighted anticipation of quitting a home which her father's increasing sottishness rendered every day more disagreeable.

"Well, then, that affair's all settled. Come to us to-morrow or next day—'twill save the trouble of sending down the posset, you know; and as you may want a trifle, perhaps, to furbish up your wardrobe, here it is—and that binds the bargain: so, there—you are regularly enlisted in my service." With these words he placed a five-pound note in her hand, and then, seating himself upon the chest, with the altered air of a man whose gracious mood was at an end, and who meant thenceforth to be rigorous and stern in his purpose, he continued—"And now tell me where *is* this precious father of yours? I must see him immediately." Overwhelmed with confusion, poor Fanny stooped down twice to pick up nothing, looked anxiously around as if in search of some missing article, felt in both her pockets, and then, resuming her seat, began to ply the empty churn with prodigious rapidity.

"You took a mug of warm milk, Squire, last time you was here," cried the mother, anxious to turn his attention and to extricate her daughter, whom she thought likely to boggle at a direct falsehood: "would you like to have another now, Sir? Here, Sally, Sally! fetch the Squire a mug of warm milk directly." Sally hastened to obey this order, in spite of Brown's surlily exclaiming—

"I don't want milk, and I do want an answer to my question. Where's your husband, Madam?"

"What, John?—what, Chubbs?—do you mean John Chubbs, Sir?" faltered the wife.

"Of course I do;—got no other husbands, have you?"

"Dear heart, Squire! the Lord forbid! Only I was just going to remark——"

"Hallo!" interposed Brown, "who is it I hear sneezing? It sounded from the chest."

"So it did, I do declare! Why, you see, Sir, our cat have kittened, and so we allow her to lie in the old chest, and she have picked up a cold somehow."

"And I should like to pick up an answer to my question—where is your husband?"

"Very true, very true: I recollect now you was a talking of my John. Why, you see, he thought Wellington were a little bit tender in the forefoot yesterday, and so he have taken him down to the farrier's, and he be always a long time a dawdling when once he do get there." The lock of the linen-chest having been wrenched off by the younger children and never replaced, there was an aperture in front, through which, at this moment, Chubbs unconsciously thrust the heated bowl of his pipe in such a way that it encountered the calf of Brown's leg.

"Zounds and the devil!" shouted the sufferer, jumping down and rubbing the part aggrieved; "does your cat bite in that way? Drown her, drown her with all her litter. I hate cats. Harkee, Madam! tell your sot of a husband that, if I am not paid my rent at the end of this quarter, I shall put an execution in the house and distrain. More than a dozen times has he promised to call upon me, and never come. The fact is, he is afraid to look me in the face, and, though he's an old soldier and a Waterloo-man, I'm sorry to say he's neither more nor less than a coward."

"That's a lie!" shouted Chubbs, throwing open the lid of the chest so suddenly that it dashed the mug out of Sally's hand as she was passing, and scattered the new milk all over Brown. "Come on, ye ly—ly—lying rascal," hiccoughed the drunken farmer, raising himself on his knees, and throwing his hands, one of which still held the pipe, into an abortive attempt at a pugilistic attitude. "I'll fi—fi—fight ye for gallon in skit—skittle-ground, Green Man."

"John, my dear John!" cried the terrified wife, putting her hand over his mouth, "for Heaven's sake hold your tongue—it's the Squire!"

"Damn the Squire!" sputtered the pot-valiant farmer through the finger-bars, at the same time throwing the pipe at his astonished landlord with a most defying air.

"O dear! O dear!" sobbed little Sally, "what will become of us all? Father has broke the mug, spilt the milk, and said a naughty word to the Squire!"

"O Sir! pray, pray forgive him," cried the wife with an appealing look: "you see, poor John don't know what he be about nor what he be a saying, no more nor a babby."

"Fanny," said Brown, nodding to the daughter, who stood weeping on the other side of her father, "don't be afraid—don't cry—I shall hold to my bargain with you: come up to the Manor-House to-morrow or next day. Mrs. Chubbs, I am sorry for you—you seem to deserve a better husband. As for you, John Chubbs, I shall let you know my mind pretty freely some other time. At present you are not yourself—you are not in your proper character—you are only a *locum tenens,* as it were."

"You're another," shouted the farmer indignantly; "and if you co—come to calling names, I'll give you as good as you bring any day in the year. Stand aside, dame, and see how I'll kno—kno—knock the fellow down." So saying, he raised his hand, and, in the effort of throwing it out, fell helplessly back in the chest, of which his wife again closed the lid, to prevent further mischief, and was about to renew her intercessions in his favour, when Brown waved his hand pettishly to silence her, and, striking his cane angrily upon the floor, hurried out of the room.

CHAPTER IX.

HAVE we not mentioned a lane, slightly diverging from the green of Wood-cote, and offering a nearer conveyance to the Manor-House? In winter-time its deep ruts rendered it hardly passable except for carts and waggons, while its pools and quagmires unfitted it for the passage of gentle feet; but in spring and summer the Shaw Lane—for thus was it called, from the little thickets that skirted it at intervals—offered a pleasant and shady walk to those who wished to avoid the dust of the high road. Partly sunk between high tufted banks pierced with occasional openings to the fields on either side, partly overshadowed by copses that completely shut out the view, it presented sufficient variety of scenery to interest the pedestrian, though its features were not more attractive than such as are commonly encountered in our rural districts.

But what is there that is not beautiful in the season of early spring? Even in the shadiest parts of the lane the tufts of May waving backwards and forwards in the wind made a light and a perfume of their own, as if they had been so many vases of incense wafted by invisible hands;—the banks and ditches were tesselated with cowslips, violets, wild hyacinths, blue germanders, foxgloves, lilies of the valley, and marsh marigolds, sometimes flaring in the ray with all the gorgeous brightness of a painted abbey-window, and in other places imparting a rich hue to the dim sunless nooks out of which they peered like so many varicoloured and rooted eyes:—butterflies spread their painted sails in the air-ocean;—the wild flowers shook on their stalks, as the bee, ceasing his murmured grace, settled upon them and commenced his honey-banquet;—the hedge-birds twittered and quivered lovingly together, or chased one another with a trembling eagerness, while the soaring lark poured down a gush of ecstasy from on high; the cattle were lowing with tranquil enjoyment amid the buttercupped and daisied herbage; the trees pushed forth their fingered leaves, and unfolded their buds, as if eager to feel and to kiss the balmy vernal air; all nature, both animate and inanimate, seemed to be thrilling with enjoyment of the season.

Men there are—we speak not of clowns and clodhoppers, but of educated and intelligent beings—who could plod upon their way along the Shaw Lane in the spring season, with little more consciousness of its beauties, because they were of an ordinary character, than the cattle which were driven along it to the farm homestead. But to him who possessed the additional and happy sense of a quick eye and apprehensive sense for the observance of natural beauties, however commonplace, the scattered copses that overhung and skirted the Shaw Lane converted it into a gallery of pictures, all executed by the same master-hand, yet ever varying in beauty and character, according to the change of position, or the play of light and shade.

Nature is an artist in whose works we can rarely detect a want of harmony, either in colour, tone, or form. Intermingled together in wild yet accordant confusion, the copses presented every variety of tint from the wan gray of the willow, the silver whiteness of the ash, and the bright green of the sycamore, to the graver hues of the beech, the elm, and the oak; while the forms varied from the spreading to the compact, from the round to the aspiring, the clumps being occasionally surmounted by a poplar, waving gracefully to and fro, like a tall feather in the leafy head-dress of nature. Nor was the symphony of sound less marked and pleasing than the concord of forms and colours—the lowing of the cows, the bleating of the sheep, and the song of the birds, blending into one choral anthem with the rustling wind; while ever and anon there broke from some mysterious distance the two fluty notes of the cuckoo, whose magic voice is always heard with a new delight, since it seldom fails to conjure up before us the pleasant recollection of our childhood.

"I have always maintained," said Walter Latimer, as he accompanied Ellen Molloy along the Shaw Lane on their way to the Manor-House, "that the spring exercises the same delightful and vivifying influence upon *us* as upon the products of the earth, making the blood in our veins dance and effervesce in merry sympathy with the sap in the trees. At all events, I can answer for my own fellow-feeling with nature, for methinks I am never so happy as in the exhilarating month of May. Not only do my intellects seem brighter, but my affections appear warmer, and those whom I always love I love still more fondly and dearly at this delicious season." As he spoke thus he gently pressed the arm of his companion, gazing upon her at the same time with all a lover's tenderness. Ellen only replied by a sigh, and her eyes, instead of reciprocating his fond regards, were bent pensively upon the ground.

"How is this?" pursued Walter; "you used, dear Ellen, to feel the cheering influence of a beautiful spring not less sensibly than myself, but for these few days past I have noticed a dejection in your manner that seems to defy all the gladdening powers of May and sunshine."

"I was in hopes you would not have observed it, dear Walter, as I have striven hard to conceal it from you, above all others; but I must confess that I have latterly been exposed to an annoyance which has distressed me more than, perhaps, it ought to have done, and which I only refrained from mentioning to you because I was in daily hopes that——"

"Nay, dear Ellen, this was hardly kind: surely the great charm of our betrothal is the perfect confidence and intercommunion of soul that it sanctions, thus enabling us to halve our sorrows and double our pleasures by sharing them with each other? And now you would withhold a vexation which I have a right to divide with you. Come, come, dearest! you must not have any reserves from me."

"Perhaps I was wrong, but, as I told you, or rather as I was about to tell you, I lived in daily hope that there would be no longer any cause for my low spirits. The fact is, dear Walter, that I have latterly been pestered with the offensive attentions and fulsome compliments of that odious Mr. Cavendish."

"What! has the insolent coxcomb again presumed to ogle you in the vulgar manner you once described, and of which, had I been with you at the time, I should certainly have expressed my opinion to him in no very measured terms?"

"Sorry am I to say that he has changed his mode of annoyance into a still more distressing one. After having so long kept aloof from my father, he has now sought his acquaintance, currying favour by sending him presents of game, or occasionally lending him a horse, and frequently calling at our cottage, when he singles me out, in a very marked manner, for his hated courtesies and unwelcome adulation."

"The saucy jackanapes! But, surely, surely, Ellen, you may put a quick end to this; you may repel and frown down his rude advances."

"Easily enough, if they were rude; but they have now become so obsequious and deferential that it is difficult to quarrel with him, which is the very reason why I think his fawning much more hateful than his free-and-easy mood. That he is utterly odious to me I take no trouble to conceal; but how can you repel a man who is studiously polite, and who will not suffer himself to be repulsed, even when you let him plainly see that his person and his pretensions, whatever they may be, are equally revolting to you?"

"Why don't you complain to your father, and request his interference?"

"Ah, dear Walter!" exclaimed Ellen, and her voice became tremulous with emotion; "would to Heaven I could do so with any prospect of success, but it is from that quarter alone that I have any misgivings, any apprehensions. Mr. Cavendish I could shake off as easily as any other noxious and crawling reptile, but my father, I grieve to say it, encourages his attentions, and positively—nay, angrily and menacingly—prohibits me from giving him his dismissal."

"Good Heavens! Ellen, you alarm me. What can the Captain mean, knowing, as he does, our solemn engagement? He would not, surely, withdraw the conditional sanction that he gave to it?"

"Alas! he now sees in it nothing but insurmountable difficulties and interminable delays. Mr. Brown, he contends, is a moody, capricious, splenetic old man, who, being unable to make up his mind as to the choice of an heir, may, probably, when he dies, leave all his money to an hospital. At all events, he feels confident that he loves his money too well to part with any of it in his lifetime; whereas Algernon Cavendish, he urges——"

"What, then! does he consider that empty-headed fop a declared suitor for your hand?"

"Not a declared but an expected one—a man who must be courted to continue his pointed attentions, until, to use my father's own words (you know his rattling way of talking), he has gone too far to recede, and must be driven, if he won't be led, into the matrimonial noose. In vain do I declare, as I have done over and over, that I loathe and despise Mr. Cavendish,—that I have bestowed my affections upon another,—that I consider you as my affianced husband. 'Tush, Nell!' he exclaims; 'Jove laughs, you know, at lovers' vows: a mere verbal engagement of this nature only stands good until a better one offers;—men jilt women, and women jilt men, every day in the year; and as to your not liking young Cavendish, what girl cares a button about the man when she can secure a brilliant settlement?' "

"I will candidly confess, dear Ellen, that I am less surprised at his thus counselling you to break your faith than at his betraying such an utter indifference to your happiness."

"But in his estimation riches and splendour *are* happiness. 'By the powers!

Nell,' has he repeatedly exclaimed to me, 'you forget what an immense catch this young fellow will prove, heir as he is to the title and large fortune of Sir Gregory, to the mansion and estate in the country, and to one of the best houses in London.' Matilda, whose lively imagination already revels in all the gaieties of the metropolis, is for ever harping upon the same discordant string; so that you cannot wonder, although I turn a deaf ear, as well as I can, to all their solicitations and worryings, that I have been unable to prevent their depressing my spirits. But why do you sigh, dear Walter, and preserve such a pensive silence? Me-thinks I might retort your charge of dejection, and accuse you of harbouring some bosom grief which you ought to have communicated to me."

"To the feeling, dearest, I will plead guilty, but not to the wish of concealing it. I was thinking—and I confess the thought was a painful one—how very little I have to offer you—I, a humble villager, and comparatively a pauper—to counterbalance the brilliant prospects which you are thus surrendering for my sake."

"Nay, dear Walter, who is unkind now? This remark was not like yourself, and it sounds, therefore, ungraciously in my ears. How very little you have to offer me! Do you not tender to me that which I prize above all earthly blessings—your own good, and gentle, and affectionate heart? And what have I—so far as worldly gifts are concerned—what have I to tender to your acceptance but——"

"The best, most charming, and most fascinating girl in the whole wide world," interposed Walter, tenderly embracing his companion.

"Well, then, if I am all-sufficient to you, do me the justice to believe that I view you in the same light, and never again venture to insinuate that, when I refuse the addresses of a rich man whom I despise, and hold fast in my affiance with a poor one whom I love, I can either feel myself, or wish to be considered by others, as making a sacrifice."

"Never again, my ever kind-hearted and generous-minded Ellen, will I revert to this subject, since it gives you pain. But still, if your constancy and truth have banished apprehension on my own account, it is most distressing to think that you should be subject to this persecution."

"That I cannot deny, for it is painful to maintain an every-day struggle with one's own family, especially when they reproach you, not only with an indifference to your own interest, but to theirs."

"Will you then, my beloved Ellen, will you promise me, if this contest becomes more urgent and annoying,—if it interferes in any way with your peace of mind and the comfort of your home,—to put an end to it at once, by consenting to our immediate marriage?"

"We shall not, I trust, be driven to any such alternative, for I hear that the Cavendish family will be shortly returning to London, and it is probable that the young coxcomb may have been only bestowing his tediousness upon me for want of a better occupation; but should any attempts be made to force him upon my acceptance, I have no hesitation in answering that I would at once accede to your proposition."

"And this you promise me—faithfully, solemnly?"

"Faithfully, solemnly, dear Walter; and there is my hand to bind the bargain."

"Ten thousand thousand thanks!" ejaculated the lover, covering her hand with kisses. "You have rolled away a stone from my heart, dearest Ellen, and have made me love you still more tenderly than before, which only half an hour ago I should have held to be impossible. As it is, I may leave Mr. Cavendish to pursue his unwelcome visits, until fashion calls him away to resume his dissipated career in the metropolis. It is no scandal, I believe, to say that he is a profligate as well as a puppy. My dear mother, ever preferring her children to herself, suggests that by laying down our little carriage I should be the better enabled to support a wife; but I would never consent, nor would you, as I well know, to deprive her of a comfort so essential to a cripple."

"Certainly not, and so I told her most explicitly when she made a similar proposition to myself."

"As to my prospects in other respects, they are not unlike the view now before us in the Shaw Lane, which is intersected here and there by bright openings, succeeded by obscurity and gloom. Do you observe that at the present moment the upper portion of our bodies catches the sloping ray of the sun, while our feet are in deep shade? Even so my head and heart have been sometimes bright with hope, as I pursued some new scheme, while the event has proved my footsteps to have been hurrying forward in the dark."

"This shows that you must not allow your hopes to travel too fast. It will be time enough to discuss our further plan of proceeding when you have obtained the situation for which you have applied."

"But, in the mean while, you will not forget your pledge as to the Cavendish persecution."

"Surely you do not doubt me already.

I have given you my promise once, and I repeat it."

"But you gave me your hand before, to bind the bargain."

"Foolish Walter! there it is again, since you require an additional security though I am half angry with you for your implied mistrust."

Ellen's beaming and affectionate looks did not support the averment, even of her half anger: Walter again covered the pledged hand with kisses, and thus the lovers pursued their way in the calm but deep felicity of mutual confidence and attachment, until they emerged from the Shaw Lane and reached the Manor-House.

Letter from Mrs. Glossop to Mrs. Jellicoe.

"Ma share Mrs. Jellicoe,

"Never was there a more complete case of *trompay voo* than when I imagined the country to be all a sort of *laissay mot tranqueel* kind of existence, where all the *paysongs* had that simplicity of character which the French so strangely term *knavetay.* Toot o contraire! *I can assure you that a* fate shampaytre *is full of the most unscrewtable* denoumongs, *and I can safely assert that the village of Woodcote, since my last letter, is more like a* coo de theatre, *than a quiet village in the* a la campagne. *First and foremost, young Allan Latimer, who was always running in master's head, so much so that it was said he had made him his hair, and who was always preambling the grounds with him, and playing at billiards, till he was quite* au naturel in the house—well, this Mr. Allan, after making *bose yew,* and sending *billy doos,* and having a regular *affair de coor* with Miss Molloy of this place, until she was dying of *amour proper* for him, ran away from Woodcote, leaving the poor girl *au comble despoir!* Was there ever such a case of cruel and deliberate *bonhommie?* If ever master did make him his hair, I'm sure he has cut him off now, for he won't hear his name mentioned. For my part, I always thought he was an impeccable *volauvong* of a fellow, and this shows that I was right. Poor Miss Molloy must cure the wound in her heart as well as she can, but I dare say it will be an eyesore as long as she lives.

"The affair of the Monk who jumped into Chubbs's cart continues in the same state of *je ne say quoi:* and Oh *ma share!* we have had another *espieglerie* still more obviously mysterious. On his return at night from a distant visit, what should master meet with in an old unfurnished house but a poor crazy mad woman, whom he brought home in the carriage, and here she has remained ever since, just as if she were *shay voo!* When we took her out all covered with blood,—for she had thrust her arms through the pains of the window,—I was in a complete state of *epouvantable,* with a *batmong de coor* in every one of my limbs; but we got her to bed, and as she was in a high fever we applied a catechism to her chest, and gave her a soaperivorous draft; and although she had already lost a good deal of blood, Dr. Dawson had recourse to further insurrection, and applied the lancet.—She passed a very restless night, which the Doctor attributed to the fleabottomy, upon which I flared up, and told him face to face,—*dos a do* as the French say,—that we had nothing of the sort in the house, and never had. The Cheltenham Doctor says it is only an extempore arrangement of her faculties, and not a case of confirmed inanity; but in the mean time her wits are quite *hore de combat,* so that it's all one and the same thing, or *two le maim* as the French say.

"Who and what she is, nobody has yet found out—*tong pea!* No doubt she has escaped from some lunar Elysium, but we can't discover it, although master has inserted advertisements every day of the week in the Gloucester 'Weekly Dispatch.' In her first dreadful state of *nonchalance* I was almost afraid to go near her, but, by struggling to become spontaneous, I have at last succeeded. People say strange things about her (*au naturel* of course), insinuating that she must have committed a *pas seul* with some one; but I do hope she is neither an *equivoke,* nor a *mauvaise honte,* nor anything of the sort, but a proper *come il fo,* for she has all the appearance of a lady. She wears a wedding-ring, which looks well; but that may be only a *double entendre* after all. She is quite a *jolly garson,*—small,—in fact, almost a *petty maitre;* but as we can't get her to *parlay voo,* we have been unable to learn anything as to her family. An audible curiosity led me to examine her clothes for marks, or the officials of her name, but I could not find anything of the sort. If we learn anything more implicit I will write to you again. In the mean time, pray don't form any injurious conclusions about the poor lady, as if she were not a *dame donneur. Honey swore key Molly paunch* is my motto, as I tell everybody that insinuates a doubt upon the subject; and I'm quite sure that you have the same *tout ensemble* as myself.

"A curious *come say drole* occurred here last week. In clearing away the ground at the foot of the old pigeon-house the workmen discovered a large stone, sculptured with figures in the very best *mauvay goo* A woman with a sword, and a youth with either a torch or a *two le maim* in his hand, are seen kneeling at the feet of an old man with a rosier on his head, holding a mitre. Some say the figures are paregorical, but it is evident, *a moi,* that they have no *savoir vivre* of the subject. To be sure I am very apt to jumble historical names and make a complete *chevoo de freeze* of my chrownology; but I do know, of course, that Joan of Arc and Guy Fawkes were the children of Cardinal Wolsey, by Mary Queen of Scots, and, *selon moi,* they are here represented kneeling at his *coo de piay* for his blessing, the sword showing Joan of Arc, and the torch Guy. It must be Cardinal Wolsey at all events, for during our sejour à Paris *we lived next door to a cemetery where they educated boys for the priesthood, so that I know the dress of the Catholic parsons and young clerks, for I used to see hundreds of them every day.* Vous savez, ma share, *that they are all doomed to sellybasy; and I'm sure it quite gave me a* mal au coor *to see so many poor little fellows, knowing that none of them could ever be enrolled in the ranks of Highmen. If I was king of France, I would immediately abolish all the conventional and bombastic houses with one* coup devil.

"Adoo, *mon share enfant gatay!* I hope you are quite *portay vous bien,* as I am at this present writing.

"*Toojoor a voo,*
"MARY GLOSSOP."

CHAPTER X.

So deep had been the disappointment of Allan Latimer when witnessing the morning rehearsal of 'Norma,' so keen his apprehensions that Isola would fail in her first assumption of the character, that he not only adhered to his resolution of absenting himself during all the subsequent rehearsals, but felt an increasing nervousness as the important night approached which was to put to so severe a test the operatic powers of his fair friend. A general and intense interest had been excited by the announcement of her first appearance in this character, many good musical judges having expressed their opinion that, with all her talents and vocal capabilities, she could hardly expect to rival, much less to eclipse, the great and gifted predecessor who had obtained such high distinction and won such universal favour by her performance of the part. Sinister whispers were afloat of her having completely broken down during the rehearsals; many, recurring to the invariable argument of the English, made bets that the manager would not renew his engagement with her after the expiration of the first limited term; jealous competitors, aggravating and repeating these rumours until they believed them, revelled in the anticipation of witnessing her downfall; and if Allan, whose admiration of Isola increased with every fresh interview, became daily more alarmed and distressed by these ominous forebodings, her own conduct was little calculated to reassure him. Although she fully admitted the great importance of the crisis, since it must accelerate or retard her return to Italy, the paramount object of all her efforts and all her wishes, her language and demeanour did not evince any correspondent anxiety to ensure success. With a ***nonchalance*** which, under such circumstances, might almost be termed a reckless levity, she only smiled and shrugged her shoulders when these evil auguries reached her ear, playfully expressing a hope that she might still be engaged as a chorus-singer, even should she be rejected as a ***prima donna;*** and anticipating with a mock solemnity the rapid falling away of her admirers and followers when she herself, no longer a fashionable operatic leader, should be lost in the subordinate train of some more successful Norma. From one circumstance alone did Allan gather any confidence. In the midst of all this seeming indifference and sportive bantering, he observed that for several hours of every morning she rigorously shut herself up, excluding all visitants, during which time, as he gathered from old Antonio, she was occupied in the incessant practice and study of her part.

Being obliged, on the anxious night of the performance, to cross the stage on his way to the box in which she had offered him a seat, Allan could not avoid noticing the altered appearance presented by everything around him. Seeing nothing of the house, for the drop-scene was down, light, order, and arrangement were everywhere substituted for the gloom and confusion he had remarked on his previous visit. On the stage he beheld the sacred forest of the Druids, with its consecrated oak in the centre, and wooded hills in the distance; while here and there emerged priests in their solemn robes, or soldiers of the Gallic army arrayed in all the pride of their barbaric panoply. But if his vision was agreeably surprised in one direction, it was painfully revolted in an opposite quarter of the stage, where was collected a little knot of dancers,—the effeminate men, rouged and whitewashed, wearing tuckered vests, and a species of short petticoat; while the females, in their nondescript costume, seemed to have consulted anything rather than the decencies of the sex.

But if he *were* shocked by their appearance alone, he was both startled and disgusted when they began to attitudenise, to spin round, to throw out and distort their limbs in the most violent postures, for no other purpose, as it appeared, than to amuse a little circle of opera frequenters, both old and young, who stood leering and smirking around them. Quitting this knot of indelicate tumblers,—for such they seemed to his unpractised eyes,—he made his way to Isola's box, which was immediately above the stage, although at some little elevation.

Amazed as he had been at the metamorphosis behind the drop-scene, the revolution in front of the house struck him with tenfold wonder. The huge dim vault, with the mysterious echoes from its undiscernible boundaries, was now transformed into a radiant and a crowded theatre, sparkling with innumerable lustres, and gay dresses, and bright-eyed beauties, while its painted dome echoed back the hum of eager voices and the preludings of the full orchestra. Even at this early hour, so great and general had been the excitement that the boxes were mostly occupied, while the pit and gallery had for some time been crowded, the prevalent subject of conversation being the chances of Isola's failure or success, which were canvassed with equal confidence by the partisans of both sides.

At length the leader of the band gave the admonitory tap with his bow, and the overture commenced, exciting perhaps less attention and admiration than on any previous night, on account of the impatience of the audience for the commencement of the opera, and the appearance of the great attraction of the night. The drop-scene rose—the Gaulish army marched upon the stage to the solemn sound of religious music, followed by a procession of Druids and priests—and Allan, hardly able to credit the evidence of his senses, so perfect and absolute was the illusion of the spectacle, felt, from the thrill of admiring wonderment that crept through his whole frame, an instant conviction that, in the mingled and exquisite delight which it pours so lavishly upon the eye and ear, no fascination can be so absorbing, so irresistible, as that of the Opera. In his instance the impression combined everything that could add to its intensity, for he was a passionate admirer of music, and this was the first time that he had ever entered a metropolitan theatre.

Shakspeare has remarked the indifference and languor that pervade an audience "after some well-graced actor leaves the stage,"—an observation equally applicable to the interval that precedes the first appearance of any celebrated performer. So it proved, at least, on the present occasion, for, though the early scenes of Norma are by no means deficient in interest, while the parts of Oroveso, Pollio, and Flavio were sustained by performers of no mean celebrity, the audience, or rather the spectators, paying but little attention to the business of the stage, were whispering to one another on the subject of Isola Guardia, or turning impatiently to the libretto, to ascertain the precise moment of her appearance. It arrived at length; and, after the first eager twittering that announced the fact, every voice was hushed,—not a fan moved,—an almost breathless silence pervaded the whole house,—and every eye of that multitudinous assemblage was gathered into one single focus.

Allan, whose anxious solicitude had been momently increasing, now felt his heart beat with a throbbing almost insupportably vehement as he riveted his gaze upon the stage. Druids, priestesses, warriors, bards, and sacrificing priests, entered in procession, and arranged themselves around the altar—there was a short pause—expectation was concentrated into intensity—a scarcely audible but thrilling hush breathed round the house; and Norma,—her exuberant dark hair hanging loose, a wreath of vervain around her brow, a golden sickle in her hand,—walked majestically forwards, seated herself on the Druidical stone, and cast a proud upbraiding look upon her silent, awe-stricken followers. From Allan's mind did that single look dispel all doubt, all fear, all misgiving, as to her conception of the character, even should her vocal powers prove inadequate to support her own lofty imaginings. Like lightning did the conviction flash upon his mind that, in the inspiration of true genius, she had undergone a temporary metempsychosis, and had infused her whole soul into the character she had assumed,—a transmigration which, by completely shutting out the audience from her thoughts and apprehensions, left her in full possession of herself and all her vocal powers.

Full, firm, sonorous, the very first sounds she uttered confirmed this impression, and it soon became a doubt which was most to be admired—the rapt, graceful, and impassioned dignity of her acting, or the exquisite and appropriate modulation of her voice. Still, however, there were many who questioned her ultimate triumph when her powers, great as they appeared in this incipient stage of the opera, should be subjected to the more trying ordeal of its later scenes: but when, as the attendant assemblage fell prostrate around her, she slowly uplifted her arms towards the full moon, and poured forth, with all the devout ardour of an inspired prophetess, the *Preghiera* of *"Casta Diva, che inargenti"* the enthusiasm of the whole audience vented itself in a burst of irrepressible delight, and all doubt of her eventual success was banished from the minds even of the most envious and sceptical.

As the first act proceeded, every fresh display of her powers was hailed with increasing fervour, especially when the devotional elevation and proud bearing which she had previously sustained were succeeded by the most feminine, the most melting, the most pathetic tenderness of look and tone, as she embraced her children, and desired her attendant to conceal them. "What an affectionate, what a doting mother would that woman make!" murmured Allan, as his thoughts almost unconsciously sounded the depths of futurity, and conjured up a vague image of a happy home, with Isola seated on one side, himself on the other, and two sweet children playing on the carpet between them. "What a marvellous power of adaptation, both in voice and feature!" he continued; "what a miraculous versatility! Who would have thought that so much feminine softness could be combined with the majestic dignity of the Druidess?"

A still more startling, but much less pleasing, change awaited him. When Norma discovers that the father of her offspring has proved false—when she seizes the arm of his guilty mistress, and in an agony of jealous rage upbraids her with her crime,—Allan found it difficult to believe that he was gazing upon the features, and listening to the tones, of the same being who had lately hung with such beaming gentleness, and poured forth such tender regrets, over her children. Changed, utterly changed, was her whole aspect. Every vein started into prominence as the blood rushed into her face and throat, her eyes flashed fire, each feature was distorted, her lips were drawn back from the teeth, like those of a wild animal about to spring upon its prey; and when, in the same scene, worked up to a paroxysm of rage, she dismisses her faithless lover with the indignant *"Vanne si; mi lascia, indegno!"* her maledictions were vented with a terrible energy that it became perfectly appalling to witness and to hear.

"Is this the kind, the gentle, the dulcet Isola?" whispered Allan, as the blood ran cold in his veins, and he strove in vain to withdraw his eyes from the contemplation of a scene that fascinated still more than it surprised him.—"Crevetti, I remember, told me that she was the daughter of a captain of banditti;—yes—yes—nothing but the fiery passions which she has inherited from a freebooter of the Abruzzi mountains could thus enable her to transform herself into a sort of Fury; but, Oh Heavens!—how beautiful is her rage! how thrilling, how sublime are the tones of this fierce anathema!"

Again, in the second act, as she raised the dagger to sacrifice her sleeping children, woke them with her shriek of horror, and then embraced them in a passion of relenting tears and tenderness, Allan's sympathising bosom was torn and convulsed by the contending emotions of terror, compassion, and deep admiration of the almost miraculous powers of the performer, who could thus adapt herself to every change with an equal intensity of feeling, and thrilling truth of representation. These emotions suffered no diminution during the remainder of the performance, which was sustained throughout with an unfailing pre-eminence of genius, and concluded amid a general and enthusiastic burst of *"Viva! Brava!"* mingled with incessant cries of *"Guardia! Guardia!"* as if the appellants supplicated her to come forward, and receive in some more pointed and emphatic manner the homage of her admirers. Long as it was continued, this hint was not taken. To Isola such public demonstrations, accompanied with the showering of premeditated wreaths, and acknowledged by humble bowings and curtsyings, appeared a humiliating act of patronage, rather than an honourable ovation. Urged as she was to confirm the favour of the audience by acceding to their wishes, she remained inflexible. Points there were, and those not trivial ones, upon which Isola might have been turned by a feather: there were others when an earthquake would not shake her indomitable resolution.

As Allan gazed round upon the brilliant and crowded audience, still evidently electrified with delight,—as he beheld the gathered aristocracy of the land, and the still nobler aristocracy of nature—the great and gifted ornaments of literature, art, and science,—all penetrated with one common feeling of admiration,—all evidently pouring forth, as they communed together, their zealous eulogies of the performer;—as Allan contemplated this flattering triumph—it might almost be said this living apotheosis of Isola, his heart swelled proudly in his bosom, and his whole soul yearned towards her with a mingled sentiment of admiration, gratitude, and affection, as he ejaculated—"And this glorious creature, this prodigy of genius, as pure in heart as she is unparagoned in talent, is, at the same time, a simple, playful, unaffected girl; and this favourite of the public, at whose feet, the proudest of the earth would be still prouder to do homage, allows me to call her my friend,—terms me her brother, her Camillo,—gives me the precious privilege of calling upon her and enjoying, as often as I like, the society of one who is not less sweet and fascinating in her sportive moods, than enlightened in her serious converse! And this very night I am permitted to sup with her, that I might endeavour to comfort her, as she jocosely said, for the failure which both her friends and enemies had been so kind as to anticipate. Truly may I deem myself a fortunate man, to be selected for such an honour, to the exclusion of others, whose rank, and station, and longer acquaintance would seem to give them a much better claim to the distinction! Happy Allan Latimer! Kind, good, and condescending Isola!"

Agitated as his bosom had been by the performance of the opera, he felt that it would be a sort of desecration to witness the afterpiece; but he had never seen anything of the sort,—it wanted yet more than an hour of the time fixed for Isola's supper; and as the ballet was reported to be got up with unusual splendour of scenery and decoration, he retained his seat until it began. Only a brief interval, however, elapsed before he quitted it, disgusted by the violent and ungraceful, as well as indelicate, distortions of the principal dancers, and not a little amazed that demure-looking mothers and modest daughters could quietly sit in the same box with sons, brothers, and admirers, to gaze upon a spectacle which to him appeared, from its licentious character, to be equally repudiated by good taste and a proper feeling of decorum.

Anxious to know how Isola had supported the fatigue and the excitement of her performance, he betook himself, on quitting the Opera House, to her residence in the Quadrant, where he learnt from Crevetti and Harry Freeman, who were already in attendance to offer their congratulations on her brilliant success, that she was lying down in her own chamber, but had sent word, by her maid, that she should shortly make her appearance. While they were yet discussing the transcendent merits of her performance she walked into the room, pale and evidently exhausted in body by the astonishing efforts she had made, but more than usually calm and self-possessed, as if resolved to show how completely she could make her well-poised mind triumph over corporeal fatigue, and its own recent excitement. "How is it, my brother, that you are here so early?" she demanded, as she smiled graciously upon Allan. "Why, you must have run away from the ballet at its very commencement,—and you told me you had never seen anything of the kind."

"Nay—do not ask me, Isola; you will think me a fool—squeamish—fastidious—puritanical; but I could not—I confess I could not bear—it appeared to me—I thought——"Allan blushed and stammered, and was unable to proceed.

"I see it—I know it—I feel it all," cried Isola: "that blush tells me that you were ashamed to gaze upon such an indecorous spectacle. Do I think you a fool for your bashful scruples? Not I indeed! No! I repeat what I have said before, that I deem one uncontaminated, delicate, and intellectual man, like my good brother Camillo, worth ten thousand of the hard-hearted, coarse-minded voluptuaries and debauchees by whom it is my unlucky fate to be usually surrounded."

"Hallo! Crevetti," cried Freeman—starting up with a look of mock indignation—"where's your castor? You and I must cut our sticks and bolt, for we are neither of us Sir Charles Grandison,—at least I can answer for myself, and I have strong doubts of you, although in dress and address you bear so startling a resemblance to that ere *preux chevalier.*"

"This is not fair," laughed Isola as she cast a glance at the somewhat shabby attire and gaunt figure of old Crevetti, whose disabled arm had increased the usual negligence of his toilet. "Present company, you know, are always excepted; and I should not have invited you to sup with me had I classed you with the roués to whom I made allusion,—those burnt-out human torches, who parade themselves offensively before us after they have lost every particle of their light and warmth. No—I have invited none of the titled or golden insolents who call themselves my personal admirers—I have asked those only whom I can respect, because they have shown a proper respect to me."

"Sir Charles Grandison!" said Freeman to Crevetti—"we may resume our seats; the Signora has bidden none to her feast but prime swells and coves of the first water; so let us hold up our heads, old boy, and make our mugs look as pretty as possible,—for handsome is as handsome does."

"Cospetto!" cried Crevetti, who had understood little or nothing of this bantering. "It is the Signora who should *andare colla testa levata*—not you and me. *Dio!* how she looked beautiful, how she played, how she sang *divinamente!* I am still *tutto stupefatto. Ecco!* I have but one hand,—this other he is *peggio che mai;* so I could not—(how you say *picchiar le mani?*)—but I cry *Bravissima!* at the top of mine voice, till I am hoarse as an old crow."

"And I," said Freeman, "clapped my hands till they are quite sore,—not with admiration, Signora, so you have thrown away that pretty smile—but with joy that you should succeed, after so many ill-natured prognostications of your failure."

"Thanks, and another smile," said Isola, holding out her hand to him. "Friendship and good wishes are ever more acceptable to me than admiration. And how did you support me, Camillo?"

"Alas! I fear but poorly," replied Allan. "I was too much rapt and absorbed to offer you any other tribute than mydeep silence, my tears, and at times my terror."

"Aha! have you then discovered that there is a devil in me, which may be conjured up by some powerful impulse? You are right, you are right! but there is also, thank Heaven! a good angel in my soul, which can control, and trample down, and enchain this evil spirit—though not always without a terrific effort. I know myself, and I suffer not my passions, if I can help it, to break from their prison."

"Since you know yourself, Isola, so well, tell me why your performance in the rehearsals was always so imperfect, so inferior, when you must have felt beforehand that your success, your glorious triumph, were placed beyond all chance or doubt?"

"Malice, nothing but malice. In certain parties both before and behind the curtain, I observed a disposition to run me down, and I fed their hopes for the moment that I might the more signally disappoint them in the end; for you must be well aware that the gratification of success arises as much—nay—sometimes more, from mortifying our enemies than pleasing our friends. Perhaps it was an unworthy *ruse de guerre,* and I am already sorry for it—but I had been ill used, and, with all my boasted command over my fierce nature, I am a dangerous person to offend."

"In this instance your revenge has been not less innocent than delightful. Yes, I perceive that your self-command is absolute in everything; otherwise, with such unlimited flexibility and power of voice, you could never have resisted the temptation of those flourishes, passages, and *roulades,* which, whether appropriate or not to the occasion and character, are sure to draw down such thunders of applause. Nothing could be more simple—I might almost say severe—than your singing in Norma, and nothing surely was ever half so effective."

"I have always consulted fitness and expression more than execution, and it might, perhaps, be as well if composers, as well as singers, would recollect a saying of my countryman Beccaria—'We pay musicians to affect and interest us, ropedancers to astonish us; and all our musicians want to be rope-dancers.' "

"He was wide awake, and no mistake, when he said that," cried Freeman. "Performers nowadays seem more anxious to conquer difficulties than to confer pleasure. Now, I hate difficulties of all sorts, and I love pleasure of all sorts; and so, my dear saltatory Sir Charles Grandison, if you feel disposed for a waltz, Harry Freeman's your partner, and we will spin round to the tune of *Vive la Bagatelle,* or Vogue la Gafère, whichever on 'em you likes."

"Venti mille diavoli!" ejaculated Crevetti, recoiling from the outstretched arms of his advancing partner. "My hand—my hand! if you touch him I go mad: he does nothing this moment but—what you call *palpita, palpita.* Dance with you! *Corpo di Bacco!* I can hardly bear my hand to sit down." Other guests now made their appearance; and, when her little party was assembled, Isola, performing the honours of the supper with a wit, cheerfulness, and sparkling vivacity that seemed stimulated rather than subdued by her previous exertions, great and trying as they had been, dismissed them at a late hour, utterly unable to decide whether she was most to be admired for her unrivalled powers as a performer and a singer, or for the mingled suavity and sprightliness that gave such an ineffable charm to every social circle graced and vivified by her presence.

CHAPTER XI.

HARRY FREEMAN was one of those frank, open-hearted, good-tempered, pleasant "fellows about town," with whom it was impossible to be only slightly acquainted. His inexhaustible good spirits—his manifest and avowed enjoyment of mere existence, apart from all its social distinctions—won upon you, even in spite of himself. The grave and squeamish soon became reconciled to his grimaces, his buffoonery, and his foolish affectation of the slang dialect. Dandies were content to overlook the capricious taste in dress which sometimes placed him in a state of contemptuous antagonism to the last prevailing mode; and even young ladies, in consideration of the general respect which he invariably evinced towards their sex, were fain to forgive him (though it is apt to be considered an irremissible offence) his uniform avoidance of all individual flirting. Many are the vulgarians whom one instantly detects, however elaborately they may attempt to act the part of gentlemen: Harry's was an opposite and less excusable ambition. It was manifest to the most casual observer that he was a real gentleman assuming the character of a vulgarian. Captivated by his inexhaustible cheerfulness, as well as by his varied talents,—for it would be difficult to mention an accomplishment of which he did not possess a smattering,—Allan Latimer's acquaintance with him quickly ripened into & considerable degree of intimacy, and became extended, by means of his introductions, to several of the most distinguished artists, literati, and men of science,—a society that he was equally proud and delighted to cultivate. Others there were, who, professing to be admirers of Allan's performance on the violoncello, or pleased with his manners and appearance, solicited introductions to him, foremost among whom was a certain Mr. Delaval, a man of fifty or upwards, who affected to be a ***fanatico per la musica,*** who dressed in the height of the fashion, sported a stylish cabriolet with a little cockaded tiger, talked familiarly of his club, of his dining with Lord George, and of his driving his friend Lord Edward down to the Opera. To Allan he had taken a great and sudden liking—it might rather be termed a sort of fatherly regard, for he gave him a world of good advice as to the dangers with which inexperienced young men are sure to be beset in London, urging his own more advanced age, and long conversancy with the snares of the metropolis, as an excuse for the liberty he was taking. Far from feeling offence—for his earnest, whispering, specious manner, as he thus enacted the part of a Mentor, was friendle almost to hugging—Allan expressed his gratitude for such useful admonitions, promising to bear them in mind should he be assailed by any of the perils and temptations against which he was thus kindly warned.

Although some time had now elapsed since Crevetti's hand had been wounded, the prospect of his recovery seemed to be more remote than ever. Fresh imposthumes formed; his general health, which was never very strong, began to give way; and he was finally ordered to the coast, for the double benefit of a change of air and of warm sea-baths. Allan, who had become attached to the kind-hearted old man, was sorry to lose him; but he kept up a correspondence with him, and regularly transmitted his share of the profits arising from the pupils, to whose tuition he had succeeded for a period that did not promise an early termination. Mr. Delaval must have been a remarkably considerate man, for he now called much more frequently than before, in order, as he said, to cheer his solitude, selecting those hours when he was sure to find him at home, and occasionally staying to sup with him, though Allan felt rather nervous at attempting to entertain a man who made no secret of his being a decided **gourmand.**

Just as he was about to leave home one morning for the purpose of giving lessons, Delaval hurried into his room, inquiring, rather anxiously, what had become of their mutual friend, honest Harry Freeman, "He started only yesterday," replied Allan, "for Elmsley Hall in Gloucestershire, where he is to take the lead in getting up some private theatricals, and where, as he told me, he was likely to be detained for a fortnight or three weeks."

"How exceedingly unfortunate!—what a very unlucky **contretemps!**" exclaimed Delaval, with a look of deep disappointment. "He is positively the only fellow of whom I would have asked such a favour,   if, indeed, that can be called a favour which is a mere matter of form."

"What is it?" inquired Allan.

"Why, I have a little bill here—an acceptance of £280—which has two or three weeks to run, and I wanted the money for it to-day, not for myself, but to oblige a friend in distress. Now, Harry would have done it in a minute."

"I doubt that; for I have heard him say that, though he has seldom twenty pounds to spare, he never owes as many shillings."

"My good fellow! do you think I would ask him for the money? not I. It is only his endorsement that I require; for though the acceptor is as good as the Bank, the over-cautious bill-broker refuses to cash it unless there are two names at the back of it,—that is to say, another besides my own."

"And will no other name than Harry Freeman's answer his purpose?"

"Oh, yes; any name in the world would do; for, as I said before, it is a mere matter of form: but I'm foolishly squeamish upon these subjects; I don't like to apply to any but fellows that I know well, and even from some of them I had much rather keep aloof. Now, there's Lord George and Lord Edward would be angry if they knew that I passed them over; but they are both chatterboxes, and I shouldn't wish the affair to be known, for with my abundant means I ought not to be in want of such a paltry sum."

"My signature, I presume, would not answer the purpose, for I am so little known in London that——"

"One name, I tell you, is as good as another; and as I am so closely pressed for time, I might, perhaps, accept your kind offer if I could be sure that you would not mention the subject to any one."

"A promise which I am quite ready to give you."

"Nay, then, in that case, I really don't see why I should not take your name as well as Harry's—it's all a form, and in my opinion a most unnecessary one. Here is the bill—regularly accepted, you see: your endorsement must come under mine, which, of course, I should not have put unless I knew the bill to be good. There, that will do. But harkye, my young friend; although it is an idle ceremony in this instance, don't do it for any one else. You might fall into bad hands—it might involve you in trouble. Mind! I depend upon your secrecy. I have not a moment to lose, so good morning." The visitant took his departure, and Allan set off to give his lessons, scarcely bestowing a second thought on what he had just done; for in his complete ignorance of business, and his confidence in Delaval, who made such a respectable appearance, and appeared to move in such elevated society, he gave implicit credence to his statements, and believed that he had performed an act of simple routine, unattended with risk or responsibility.

On the following morning he received a hurried note from that worthy, stating that he was obliged to go out of town for a few days in order to liberate his friend from his difficulties, and was uncertain as to the precise moment of his return,—a communication which explained his non-appearance for the next fortnight. Two days after the expiration of that period, Allan was not less surprised than alarmed at receiving a visit from an undersized, sinister-looking man of law, dressed in rusty black, who drew out the acceptance from a leathern case and demanded payment of 280*l.*, with some trifling addition for notarial charges, the bill having been protested for non-payment by the acceptor. "Good Heavens!" ejaculated Allan, colouring with apprehension; "you surely do not expect *me* to pay it!—I have no means in the world of doing so,—I was assured that the acceptor was as good as the Bank. You must look to Mr. Delaval."

"Much use in that!" replied the claimant with a grim smile. "Get but little tin from him at any time, and just now I suspect he's playing at hide and seek."

"Ought you not then to proceed against the acceptor."

"Not if we look for payment, for he's little better than a man of straw. You see, Sir, I act for Mr. Smales, the discounter and holder of the bill, who may pounce upon the acceptor or drawer, or either of the endorsers, just as he thinks fit; and he chooses to select you, and has given me orders to proceed against you with all possible rigour, so that I should strongly recommend you to pay the money, or I must take out a writ, and proceed to extremities, which is always exceedingly painful to my feelings, as it must be, in course, to any gentleman of fine——"A long yawn, followed by an indolent stretching of the arms, prevented the completion of the sentence.

"Will you allow me to observe that this is very unhandsome conduct on the part of Mr. Smales?"

"Oh, certainly, certainly, Sir! I will allow anything you wish, except any delay in the payment of the bill, upon which subject my orders are peremptory."

"But I have no means of paying it—none in the world."

"Nothing more likely; there are many others in the same predicament; but we are advised that you have friends quite competent, and I dare say willing, to assist you,—Mr. Freeman, for instance; the old music-master, who is reported to be worth money; and the. Italian singing-woman, who must be picking up the cash as fast as she can count it. They say you are her fancy-man, and if so, such a trifle as this can never——"

"I must desire, Sir, that you will not make any disrespectful allusion to Signora Guardia, if your coarse insinuations point towards that lady."

"What! that affair's all upon the sly, is it? Well, Sir, well, just as *you* please, but for such a trifling amount, and with such good friends——"

"But I have not the smallest right to apply to any of those parties, nor would I do so on any consideration; besides, they are all absent from London,—the Signora having started two or three days ago for the great musical festival in the North: which circumstances, if they were made known to Mr. Smales, would surely induce him to forego his claim."

"Oh, come, hang it! you can't be so green as all that! And if you are, it may be right to tell you that my client is a particularly rum customer, and won't stand any nonsense; so that, if the money, for the acceptance, the notary's process, and my little bill of costs, isn't sent to me before to-night (here's my card of address), the writ will issue instantly."

"And what will be the consequence?" The man of law looked at his interrogator with a contemptuous sneer, as if doubting whether the question were put mockingly or in simple ignorance; but having quickly decided in favour of the latter predicament, strange as it seemed to him, he replied, with a blander expression, "Why, my very good Sir, in the first instance you'll be arrested and taken to a lo— o—o—ock-up-house (a yawn lengthened out the beginning of the word); and if you can't pay or get bail, you must go to—(yaw—aw—haw!) quod—which, as I said before, would be very painful to a gentleman of my fine—(yaw—aw—haw!) I hardly got any sleep last night—that under-sheriff is the devil's own fellow for brandy-and-water and cigars; and so, Sir, I wish you a very good morning. Take care of the card."

"One word before you go. I must look to Mr, Delaval, who has behaved very unhandsomely to me in this affair. Where shall I be likely to find him?"

"Nowhere just now; he's a dodger for the present, as I told you before."

"But who is he? What is he?"

"A flat-catcher, *we* call him. But he's not so bad as some. He pays very honourably when he's flush, but that is not the case just now, or he wouldn't be flying kites." With these words the unwelcome visitant gave a familiar nod, as a substitute for a bow, and disappeared, leaving Allan to reflect upon the probable consequences of the dilemma in which he was placed, and from which he did not perceive any immediate mode of extrication. His predominant feeling was one of bitter indignation against the pretended friend by whom he had been so insidiously duped and betrayed; but this gradually subsiding, as the natural generosity of his own disposition suggested that Delaval, after all, might have thought the acceptor a solvent man, he began to consider what chances he had of procuring the money, so as to avoid the disgrace as well as the serious injury of an arrest. His detention, for however short a period, would entail the certain loss of the pupils whom he was now holding together for Crevetti's advantage as well as his own,—to say nothing of the dishonour, which assumed a much more alarming and degrading aspect to his inexperienced mind than it would have presented to a practised man of fashion.

That his arrest should come to the knowledge of Isola, and of others whose good opinion he was equally anxious to conciliate, was a contingency which he contemplated with feelings of the deepest shame and repugnance. But by what means could he avoid it? A sale of a portion of the stock which constituted his little property would doubtless enable him to pay the amount; but it stood in the joint names of himself and his brother, so that he could do nothing without making known to his family the humiliating position in which he was placed, and distressing the mother to whom he was so affectionately devoted,—an alternative which he could not bear to think of, even for an instant. Mr. Lum was the only man of business with whom he had the slightest acquaintance; but he had been so cavalierly treated by him, that he had little reason to expect any friendly offices in that quarter; and he wished, moreover, to avoid being interrogated on the subject of Jemima's projected elopement with Captain Harcourt, as he had promised never to reveal her indiscretion to her austere father.

The result of all these unsatisfactory self-communings was a determination to find out Delaval, if possible, and, if not, to write him a letter, insisting upon his immediate payment of the bill; and at the same time to solicit from Mr. Smales, the holder of the acceptance, a delay of a few days. Of the former gentleman he could gather no tidings, nor was time allowed for obtaining a reply to the letter left at his lodgings, even had it been forwarded to him, for Allan was arrested the next morning, and conveyed to a lock-up-house in Cursitor Street, the gloomy aspect of which was little calculated to dispel the deep dejection that now oppressed his soul. Guiltless as he was of all offence, beyond that of a very venial indiscretion, he imagined that an indelible infamy would attach to him should he be conveyed to a public prison; and even his present place of confinement, with the two well-secured and carefully guarded doors through which he had passed in the passage, and the iron-barred window of the narrow room upon the ground-floor to which he was inducted, making him look upon himself as a criminal, stung him with a mingled anguish of humiliation and abhorrence.

Justly proud of the unspotted name he had hitherto preserved, and apprehensive of the injurious and false constructions which might be put upon his incarceration, he became every moment more anxious to conceal it, and less able to discern any mode whereby his public exposure could be avoided; in which conflict of emotions he sat for more than an hour, plunged in a deep and inconsolable perplexity, which, so far from allowing him to devise any scheme for his present conduct or ultimate extrication, hardly left him in possession of his senses. Rallying his faculties at length from this stupor, he wrote in the first instance to Crevetti, detailing what had occurred, after which he indited a still more urgent letter to Delaval, repeating his utter inability to find funds for the payment of this unexpected demand; and finally, though not without many scruples, he forwarded by post a few lines to Harry Freeman, stating what had passed at the time of the interview with Delaval, as well as the painful result to which it had led, and soliciting his advice as to what course of action it would be most prudent to adopt.

Tranquillised in some degree by this employment of his mind, he took up an old newspaper, smelling strongly of tobacco, which was lying on the table, endeavouring to interest himself in its contents, that so he might be abstracted from his own melancholy thoughts. Instead of succeeding in this object, although his eyes remained fixed upon the journal, he sank into a gloomy reverie of long continuance, until he was aroused by the delivery of a letter which had arrived at his lodgings immediately after his departure, and had been forwarded by the landlady, who knew his present address from having heard the orders given to the hackney-coachman, as he was driven away in company with the bailiffs. Recognising the handwriting of Walter, he tore it open, and read as follows:—

"Woodcote, Tuesday.

"MY DEAR ALLAN!

"Our beloved mother was seized three hours ago with a most alarming fit! God knows whether she will ever recover. At present she is speechless; but she retains her faculties, for she has just written with pencil the words—'Send instantly for Allan—I must see him before I die.' You had better come down *immediately.* Nevertheless, I will write again to-morrow. I have no time to add more.

"Yours, in the deepest affliction,

"WALTER LATIMER.

"P.S.—I have broken open the letter to say that Dawson thinks we need not by any means despair, should there be no *second* attack. W. L."

As he finished the perusal of these heart-rending lines, the letter dropped from his grasp, and the tears rained upon his folded hands, while he sat with his eyes fixed upon the floor in a mute agony of grief. Starting from this prostration of mind, he snatched up the letter, and essayed to read it a second time, to see whether its reperusal might afford him a faint ray of hope; but he was so blinded by his tears, and his hand so tremulous with agitation, that he could not at first succeed; nor, when he had at length accomplished his purpose, could he find anything to alleviate the pang of wretchedness, the unutterable misery with which he was overwhelmed. Now did he recall with bitter self-upbraidings that he had left Woodcote without receiving his mother's parting blessing, without even bidding her adieu; and, although he had constantly written to her since his arrival in London, his conscience stung him as if he had been the most negligent, the most unfilial, the most unnatural, of sons.

"And this kindest, best, most affectionate of mothers," exclaimed Allan, smiting his forehead in a paroxysm of accusing penitence, "not only forgives my unkindness in quitting my home, but thinks of me before all others when she is suddenly hurried to the brink of the grave, and declares that she must see me before she dies. And this, as if on purpose to accumulate horrors upon my unhappy head, this is made known to me when I am locked up in prison like a felon—when I must leave her to suppose that her dying request was unheeded by her ungrateful son,—that I, upon whom she has never gazed except with a smile of tenderness—I, whom she has so carefully reared—I, whom she has ever so fondly loved——By Heaven! I must, I will fly to her bedside—nothing—no consideration on earth shall prevent me!"

Thus soliloquising, while he rapidly paced the room in a state of intense excitement, he suddenly threw up the sash, and made a violent wrench at one of the iron bars, in the hope of displacing it; but, finding it as immovable as the house itself, he stamped upon the floor with a feeling of mortification that now amounted to rage. In the midst of his exacerbation, a thought occurred to him, or rather a chimera, which could only have been suggested by despair acting upon inexperience. He closed the sash, pulled the bell, and desired to speak to the master of the house, on the appearance of which functionary, a tall, raw-boned man of a most forbidding aspect, he placed the letter in his hand, desired him to read it, and then, adjuring him by his love of his own mother if she were still living, by his respect for her memory if she were dead, by every consideration of Christian charity, he implored permission, in the most impassioned tones, to hurry down by that night's mail-coach to Woodcote, that he might receive his mother's blessing, solemnly swearing that he would return in two days, and again place himself in safe custody.

Difficult would it be to describe the scorn, surprise, and wrath, mingled in the countenance of the party thus addressed, as he replied, "Why, what a precious jackass you must think me! Do I look so jolly green, such a downright dummy, as all that comes to? Call me away from my brandy-and-water, and my game of cribbage, to try and come over me with a parcel of living mothers, and dying mothers, and dead mothers, and blessings, and such rubbish as that! Curse me if ever I met with a bigger piece of gammon in all my life!"

"Nay, for pity's sake! for Heaven's sake! do not leave me. If you will but grant my request, I swear to you, by all that is great and good—all that is sacred——"

"Humbug!" exclaimed the fellow, rudely shaking off the petitioner, who endeavoured to detain him by the arm, and banging the door after him, as he flounced angrily out of the room.

"Then there is no hope!" groaned Allan, as he threw himself into a chair, buried his face in his hands, and sobbed in a burst of uncontrollable despair. So absorbing was his distress that he did not notice an altercation in the passage, until it became so clamorous and turbulent as to force itself upon his attention. On quitting the little back room in the manner we have described, the sheriffs officer discovered that the janitor, who had a seat inside the second door of the passage, was not only fast asleep upon his post, but that, when he was aroused, by no very gentle shake, he was much too drunk to be left as the custodian of the house. He accordingly summoned another of his myrmidons from below to take the place of the delinquent,—a substitution which the latter resisted with so much violence, that his two assailants found considerable difficulty in forcing him from his post, and dragging him below, preparatory to his being locked up in the back kitchen until he should recover his sobriety.

While they were yet scuffling and wrangling together upon the stairs, Allan opened the room-door in order to ascertain the cause of the disturbance; and, seeing the coast clear, the possibility of making his escape flashed athwart his mind with all the speed of lightning. Hurrying forward upon tiptoe, he turned the key of the inner door, which had been left in the lock, and with a thrilling bosom reached the intermediate passage; but his blood again ran cold with a blank and deadly misgiving as he perceived that there was no key to the outer door, which was securely locked. Not wishing to be detected in a vain attempt to escape, and well aware that there was not a moment to be lost, he was on the point of hurrying back to his place of confinement, when it struck him that the same key might possibly open both doors. Withdrawing it from the first, he inserted it noiselessly in the second lock; he turned it; the bolts receded; he opened the outer door, closing it softly behind him; and, while his heart gave a leap as if it would have sprung from his bosom, he found himself in the street, and at liberty.

Agile and quick-footed at all times, his speed was now that of a flying antelope; the buoyancy of his spirit seemed to have given levity to his whole frame; and his feet scarcely touched the ground till he plunged into a crowded thoroughfare, where he was compelled to check the rapidity of his progress. Again would he have turned aside into some of the less-frequented streets, but, recollecting that, should he be pursued, he had a better chance of avoiding detection in a crowd, he continued his course, restricting his advance to a quick walk. As he had shut the door of his little room on making his escape, as well as both those in the passage, he flattered himself that his flight might not be discovered for some time; and even if it were, nothing was so improbable as that he should be again apprehended before he reached the Post-Office, where he hoped to find the mail. He had now obtained a good start; his pursuers would be utterly ignorant of the direction he had taken; and he felt no compunction or alarm as to the possible consequences of his evasion, since he fully intended to replace himself in custody the very moment that he should be enabled to return from Woodcote.

With these consolatory impressions he hastened forwards to the Post-Office, where he was informed that an hour would elapse before the arrival and departure of the mail. Small as was the chance of his discovery during that short period, he determined not to incur any unnecessary risk, but ensconced himself in the darkest corner of an obscure coffee-house, where he called for some refreshment, although he was too much agitated to taste it when it was placed before him. Emerging from this retreat as the appointed time drew nigh, he returned to the Post-Office, and was looking out for the coach he wanted, when, to his utter horror and amazement, his eyes fell upon the tall, raw-boned sheriffs officer from whose house he had so recently made his escape. That crafty personage, recollecting the eager and repeated declarations of his prisoner that he wished to travel to Woodcote by that night's mail, had no sooner been apprised of his elopement than he judged that the most likely chance for effecting his recaption was to lie in wait for him at the Post-Office, and the result proved that he had not been mistaken. His suspicious, peering eye having instantly detected the runaway, his long legs were in strenuous pursuit when Allan commenced his second flight, which he did with a velocity not less vehement than the first.

Fortunately for the fugitive, it was a wet, foggy evening; and as he darted down a narrow street, ignorant whither it might lead him, none of the few wayfarers offered to interrupt his passage, although his pursuer repeatedly and lustily shouted "Stop thief!"—Active as he was, however, Allan had presently the mortification to find that his follower was gaining upon him; he could hear his footsteps and his outcries at no great distance behind;—and as he rushed through a narrow covered passage by which he was momentarily concealed, and emerged into an obscure alley, he bolted into a house the door of which stood ajar, and instantly closed it, hoping that the party who held him in chase would continue his precipitous career without suspecting the stratagem. To his immeasurable relief of mind, he heard him hurry past the door, and listened to his receding footsteps and fainter cries until both became inaudible, when, deeming himself safe for the immediate moment, he prepared to leave the house and run back to the Post-Office, in the hope of still being in time for the coach.

At this instant several of the neighbouring church clocks struck the hour of eight,—sounds which fell heavily upon his heart, for he knew that he had now lost all hope of leaving London by that night's mail. Having thus no object to urge him forth from his present place of concealment, which seemed a quiet and secure one, the house appearing to be unoccupied, he determined to lie *perdu* a little longer, deeming it by no means impossible that the sheriffs officer, turning upon his steps, might prowl about the neighbourhood in the hope of pouncing a second time upon his prey.

Just as he was at length about to quit the premises, he heard two men whispering together outside the door, one of whom placed his hand upon the lock as if about to enter, and his heart again sank within him, for he feared that his adversary had discovered his place of concealment; with which impression he stole stealthily up the stairs, and, looking into a back room upon the first floor, was enabled to discern by the dim light of its single window,—for night was now setting in,—that it contained no furniture except a table in the centre, and that there was a closet in the farther corner. To this he crept, and drew the door gently after him, intending to wait until the men below, whose visit to an unfurnished house was not likely to be of long continuance, should have taken their departure. It was some comfort to conclude that they were not in pursuit of him, since they made no attempt to search the premises, or even to ascend the stairs; but, on the other hand, they evinced no disposition to depart, for the fumes of tobacco penetrated to his closet, and he caught their voices at intervals, although his eager ears were unable to distinguish a single word of their discourse, so low was the tone in which they conversed. From the total absence of any sound of wheels in the alley, he concluded that it was not a thoroughfare for carriages, and he almost wished that he could have heard their rumbling, so trying to his nerves became the mysterious whispering of these strangers, such an evil purpose might fairly be implied from the circumstances of their meeting, and so completely did he feel himself in their power.

After a delay of some continuance, which appeared still longer from the impatient agitation of his mind, he heard the rolling as of a barrow without; it stopped—two taps were given to the door, which was immediately opened; additional voices, but still in the same earnest, subdued, whispering tone, buzzed upwards from the passage; and in another minute Allan felt a thrill of alarm tingling through his whole frame as several footsteps were heard treading heavily Tip the creaking stairs. And yet, he argued to himself—for in any crisis of danger the operations of the electrified mind are carried on with an inconceivable rapidity—I have no reason to suppose that these men are aware of my presence; I have only to remain quiet, and in all probability I shall not be discovered;—they may not be employed on any lawless purpose; and if they are, and should chance to ferret me out, I am young and strong, and shall have the less reason to fear them, for the guilty are always cowards. While these thoughts were flashing across him, the door opened, and he became conscious that a light had been introduced into the room, for a ray gleamed into the closet through a circular hole occasioned by the dropping of a knot from the deal door. By looking through this aperture, small as it was, he could see everything that passed in the room, without being himself detected; and an irresistible curiosity having presently riveted his eye to the minute opening, he saw that three suspicious-looking fellows had entered the room, one of them bearing a sack upon his shoulders which he threw upon the table, exclaiming, as he wiped the perspiration from his brow with the sleeve of his fustian coat—"Curse the cove! who'd ha' thought he was so heavy? A precious trundle I've had with the barrow. He warn't an easy go-a-longer, I can tell you that; but your dead uns are always as lumpy as blue pigeon. Jemmy! you've brought some lush, some regular max, ha'n't you? for I've had no grub since we started."

"Stow that," replied the man thus addressed—"we'll have a regular blow out by and bye. Hide the glim, spoony! don't you see there's a glaze?" And he pointed to the window.

"It's a back slum, and looks out upon a dead wall."

"That's it, and no mistake; then we'll have t'other glim, that we may see what we're about." With these words he turned back the shade of a dark lantern, and, placing it upon the narrow mantel, so that its light fell upon the table, he continued—"Come, my hearties! stir your stumps: we've no me to lose—open the sack, kiddy! and out with him." The sack was untied, when Allan, shuddering with horror, saw a dead body unceremoniously dragged forth and stretched upon the table, while one of the men, who by his dress seemed to be a sort of leader, bowing to the corpse with a mock solemnity, exclaimed—"Your sarvant, Captain; you're out of twig just now, but we'll soon make a prime swell of you."

"What dark and atrocious deed have these miscreants been committing?" thought Allan: "they may be murderers, and I perchance may be the destined instrument of Providence for detecting their guilt and bringing the villains to justice." In this belief he fixed his eyes upon the faces of each in succession, that he might swear to their identity, should he become a witness against them; during which scrutiny a momentary silence in the room thrilled him with a fresh alarm, for he heard with a painful distinctness the ticking of his own watch, and had too much reason to fear, should the sound lead to his discovery, that the desperadoes, endeavouring to secure the concealment of one crime by the commission of another, would put him to death in a sort of self-defence. In the rapid flashes of thought, snatching at safety as eagerly as it conjured up ideas of danger, it now occurred to him that the men, after all, might be only body-snatchers, who had exhumed a corpse for anatomical purposes,—a supposition which brought such a relief to his mind that he could almost have smiled at his own previous terrors and misgivings.

This illusion was, however, dispelled still more quickly than it had been formed, for, a parcel of clothes being emptied upon the floor from another bag, the leader of the party proceeded to array the corpse, calling for the different articles of dress as he required them. "Is all the toggery right?" was his first question; to which an affirmative answer having been given, the body was carefully dressed in what appeared to be a handsome and fashionable suit of clothes. "Now for the jasey and the castor," said the mysterious valet, placing a wig and hat upon the head of the deceased. "There you are, Captain," he continued—"togg'd out to the nines, and as prime a swell as e'er a flashman in London; so now, my lads, we'll just have a snatch at the prog down-stairs, and whet our whistles,—for this dead-man's work rather turns a fellow's stomach,—and then we'll make a fresh start."

"And when are we to share the swag?" asked one of his companions. "All in good time, Jemmy; it's a prime stake, depend on't, and there'll be lots of blunt for all of us, if nobody blows the gaff. If they do, and we're all in the same boat, it's a lagging matter at the least." To the inexpressible relief of their closeted observer, the party now went downstairs, taking with them the candle, but leaving the dark-lantern on the mantelshelf; and their voices were again indistinctly heard from below, as they discussed the viands and the liquor to which one of them had made allusion.

Allan was now more bewildered than ever as to what course he should pursue. Prudence, not to say the possible chance of self-preservation, suggested that he should seize the moment while they were engaged with their meal for stealing down-stairs and attempting to quit the house without discovery; but, on the other hand, an irrepressible curiosity to witness the conclusion of the adventure, and a brave feeling that his duty to the public required him to ascertain, if possible, its object, and the names of the agents engaged in so suspicious a transaction, incited him to remain.

Little conversant as he was with the slang language, he had gathered enough from the lips of the last speaker to feel assured that he had been engaged in some nefarious deed which would subject himself and his fellows to a heavy punishment if it should ever be revealed,—an admission which strengthened his desire to solve its mystery, and assist in the conviction of the culprits. While thus communing with himself, he felt vehemently tempted to quit his hiding-place for a single moment, that he might take a survey of the body, his present line of vision only allowing him to see the back part of the head as it lay extended before him. Recollecting that his footsteps were not likely to be heard by the party below, who were in the front room, and busily engaged with their potations, he summoned courage, stole from the closet, took the lantern in his hand, and, holding it full in the face of the deceased, started back in utter amazement as his eyes fell upon the form and features of Captain Harcourt, whose intended elopement with Jemima Lum he had so recently frustrated. At that time he had appeared in perfect health, and, though the closed eyes and the cadaverous hues of death made some alteration in his appearance, there could be no question as to his identity, the singular scar upon his cheek and throat being now more conspicuous than ever, while his clothes, remarkable for their peculiar cut and colour, were obviously the same that he had worn on that occasion.

Considering himself to be holding a sort of inquest on the body, Allan made no scruple of feeling in the coat-pockets, whence he drew several letters, all directed to "Captain Harcourt, Hill Street, Richmond,"—as well as a silver-mounted case, filled with cards bearing the same name and address. As he hastily returned these to the pockets, his eye fell upon a handsome chain,—he drew forth the watch to which it was appended, and read the same words engraved upon the outer case.

One of the dead man's fingers bore a showy ring, which he also wished to examine, but, revolted by the cold, clammy feeling of the hand, and recoiling from the very notion of tampering any longer with a corpse, he gave up the attempt, and, being quite satisfied as to the identity of the party, hurried back to his lair.

Fortunate was it that he did so, for footsteps were immediately afterwards heard ascending; the three men reappeared, flushed with their recent potations, and, replacing the dressed body in the sack which had brought it, not without sundry coarse and unfeeling jokes as to the flashy appearance of the Captain, they carried it down-stairs, where, as Allan conjectured, they again consigned it to the barrow, for he could distinguish the trundling of its receding wheel. Eager to fathom the mystery, he was about to follow in instant pursuit, when he found that the men had not all quitted the house,—a noise, as if of packing up the drinking-vessels that had been used, still proceeding from the lower room. Knowing that discovery would effectually defeat his purpose, he waited until these sounds had subsided, when he crept noiselessly down the stairs, gently opened the street door, which had been left unfastened, and found himself in the alley, hardly able to explore his way, so dark was the foggy night, and so few the lamps in that obscure and neglected passage. Pressing, however, forwards in the direction that the barrow had taken, so far as he could judge by the sound, and flattering himself that, as his movements were quicker, he must soon overtake it, he presently emerged into a wider and better lighted street, which crossed the alley at right angles. Here he remained listening, utterly at a loss which way to turn, especially when a passing watchman declared, in answer to his inquiries, that, although he had been pacing up and down for some time, he had neither seen a barrow nor encountered any suspicious characters. Unsatisfied with this reply, Allan hurried along the pavement to some distance, first in one direction, then in the other; but, not succeeding in the object of his search, though it was continued until the tolling of the midnight hour, he gave up the pursuit, turned into a coffee-house that he found still open, and engaged a bed, to which he retired, completely exhausted, both in mind and body, by the strange adventures which had crowded more distress, excitement, and mysterious wonder into the last few hours than it had been his lot to experience in the whole course of his previous life.

END OF VOL. II.

The Codes Of Hammurabi And Moses
W. W. Davies

The discovery of the Hammurabi Code is one of the greatest achievements of archaeology, and is of paramount interest, not only to the student of the Bible, but also to all those interested in ancient history...

Religion   **ISBN:** *1-59462-338-4*

QTY

Pages:132
MSRP $12.95

The Theory of Moral Sentiments
Adam Smith

This work from 1749. contains original theories of conscience amd moral judgment and it is the foundation for systemof morals.

Philosophy **ISBN:** *1-59462-777-0*

QTY

Pages:536
MSRP $19.95

Jessica's First Prayer
Hesba Stretton

In a screened and secluded corner of one of the many railway-bridges which span the streets of London there could be seen a few years ago, from five o'clock every morning until half past eight, a tidily set-out coffee-stall, consisting of a trestle and board, upon which stood two large tin cans, with a small fire of charcoal burning under each so as to keep the coffee boiling during the early hours of the morning when the work-people were thronging into the city on their way to their daily toil...

Childrens   **ISBN:** *1-59462-373-2*

QTY

Pages:84
MSRP $9.95

My Life and Work
Henry Ford

Henry Ford revolutionized the world with his implementation of mass production for the Model T automobile. Gain valuable business insight into his life and work with his own auto-biography... "We have only started on our development of our country we have not as yet, with all our talk of wonderful progress, done more than scratch the surface. The progress has been wonderful enough but..."

Biographies/   **ISBN:** *1-59462-198-5*

QTY

Pages:300
MSRP $21.95

The Art of Cross-Examination
Francis Wellman

I presume it is the experience of every author, after his first book is published upon an important subject, to be almost overwhelmed with a wealth of ideas and illustrations which could readily have been included in his book, and which to his own mind, at least, seem to make a second edition inevitable. Such certainly was the case with me; and when the first edition had reached its sixth impression in five months, I rejoiced to learn that it seemed to my publishers that the book had met with a sufficiently favorable reception to justify a second and considerably enlarged edition. ..

QTY

Pages:412

Reference   ISBN: *1-59462-647-2*   *MSRP $19.95*

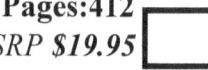

On the Duty of Civil Disobedience
Henry David Thoreau

Thoreau wrote his famous essay, On the Duty of Civil Disobedience, as a protest against an unjust but popular war and the immoral but popular institution of slave-owning. He did more than write—he declined to pay his taxes, and was hauled off to gaol in consequence. Who can say how much this refusal of his hastened the end of the war and of slavery ?

QTY

Law   ISBN: *1-59462-747-9*   **Pages:48**

MSRP $7.45

Dream Psychology Psychoanalysis for Beginners
Sigmund Freud

Sigmund Freud, born Sigismund Schlomo Freud (May 6, 1856 - September 23, 1939), was a Jewish-Austrian neurologist and psychiatrist who co-founded the psychoanalytic school of psychology. Freud is best known for his theories of the unconscious mind, especially involving the mechanism of repression; his redefinition of sexual desire as mobile and directed towards a wide variety of objects; and his therapeutic techniques, especially his understanding of transference in the therapeutic relationship and the presumed value of dreams as sources of insight into unconscious desires.

QTY

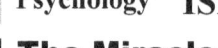

Pages:196

Psychology   ISBN: *1-59462-905-6*   *MSRP $15.45*

The Miracle of Right Thought
Orison Swett Marden

Believe with all of your heart that you will do what you were made to do. When the mind has once formed the habit of holding cheerful, happy, prosperous pictures, it will not be easy to form the opposite habit. It does not matter how improbable or how far away this realization may see, or how dark the prospects may be, if we visualize them as best we can, as vividly as possible, hold tenaciously to them and vigorously struggle to attain them, they will gradually become actualized, realized in the life. But a desire, a longing without endeavor, a yearning abandoned or held indifferently will vanish without realization.

QTY

Pages:360

Self Help   ISBN: *1-59462-644-8*   *MSRP $25.45*

QTY

The Rosicrucian Cosmo-Conception Mystic Christianity *by Max Heindel*   ISBN: *1-59462-188-8*   **$38.95**
The Rosicrucian Cosmo-conception is not dogmatic, neither does it appeal to any other authority than the reason of the student. It is: not controversial, but is: sent forth in the, hope that it may help to clear...   New Age/Religion Pages 646

Abandonment To Divine Providence *by Jean-Pierre de Caussade*   ISBN: *1-59462-228-0*   **$25.95**
"The Rev. Jean Pierre de Caussade was one of the most remarkable spiritual writers of the Society of Jesus in France in the 18th Century. His death took place at Toulouse in 1751. His works have gone through many editions and have been republished...   Inspirational/Religion Pages 400

Mental Chemistry *by Charles Haanel*   ISBN: *1-59462-192-6*   **$23.95**
Mental Chemistry allows the change of material conditions by combining and appropriately utilizing the power of the mind. Much like applied chemistry creates something new and unique out of careful combinations of chemicals the mastery of mental chemistry...   New Age Pages 354

The Letters of Robert Browning and Elizabeth Barret Barrett 1845-1846 vol II   ISBN: *1-59462-193-4*   **$35.95**
by Robert Browning and Elizabeth Barrett   Biographies Pages 596

Gleanings In Genesis (volume I) *by Arthur W. Pink*   ISBN: *1-59462-130-6*   **$27.45**
Appropriately has Genesis been termed "the seed plot of the Bible" for in it we have, in germ form, almost all of the great doctrines which are afterwards fully developed in the books of Scripture which follow...   Religion/Inspirational Pages 420

The Master Key *by L. W. de Laurence*   ISBN: *1-59462-001-6*   **$30.95**
In no branch of human knowledge has there been a more lively increase of the spirit of research during the past few years than in the study of Psychology, Concentration and Mental Discipline. The requests for authentic lessons in Thought Control, Mental Discipline and...   New Age/Business Pages 422

The Lesser Key Of Solomon Goetia *by L. W. de Laurence*   ISBN: *1-59462-092-X*   **$9.95**
This translation of the first book of the "Lernegton" which is now for the first time made accessible to students of Talismanic Magic was done, after careful collation and edition, from numerous Ancient Manuscripts in Hebrew, Latin, and French...   New Age/Occult Pages 92

Rubaiyat Of Omar Khayyam *by Edward Fitzgerald*   ISBN:*1-59462-332-5*   **$13.95**
Edward Fitzgerald, whom the world has already learned, in spite of his own efforts to remain within the shadow of anonymity, to look upon as one of the rarest poets of the century, was born at Bredfield, in Suffolk, on the 31st of March, 1809. He was the third son of John Purcell...   Music Pages 172

Ancient Law *by Henry Maine*   ISBN: *1-59462-128-4*   **$29.95**
The chief object of the following pages is to indicate some of the earliest ideas of mankind, as they are reflected in Ancient Law, and to point out the relation of those ideas to modern thought.   Religion/History Pages 452

Far-Away Stories *by William J. Locke*   ISBN: *1-59462-129-2*   **$19.45**
"Good wine needs no bush, but a collection of mixed vintages does. And this book is just such a collection. Some of the stories I do not want to remain buried for ever in the museum files of dead magazine-numbers an author's not unpardonable vanity..."   Fiction Pages 272

Life of David Crockett *by David Crockett*   ISBN: *1-59462-250-7*   **$27.45**
"Colonel David Crockett was one of the most remarkable men of the times in which he lived. Born in humble life, but gifted with a strong will, an indomitable courage, and unremitting perseverance...   Biographies/New Age Pages 424

Lip-Reading *by Edward Nitchie*   ISBN: *1-59462-206-X*   **$25.95**
Edward B. Nitchie, founder of the New York School for the Hard of Hearing, now the Nitchie School of Lip-Reading, Inc, wrote "LIP-READING Principles and Practice". The development and perfecting of this meritorious work on lip-reading was an undertaking...   How-to Pages 400

A Handbook of Suggestive Therapeutics, Applied Hypnotism, Psychic Science   ISBN: *1-59462-214-0*   **$24.95**
by Henry Munro   Health/New Age/Health/Self-help Pages 376

A Doll's House: and Two Other Plays *by Henrik Ibsen*   ISBN: *1-59462-112-8*   **$19.95**
Henrik Ibsen created this classic when in revolutionary 1848 Rome. Introducing some striking concepts in playwriting for the realist genre, this play has been studied the world over.   Fiction/Classics/Plays 308

The Light of Asia *by sir Edwin Arnold*   ISBN: *1-59462-204-3*   **$13.95**
In this poetic masterpiece, Edwin Arnold describes the life and teachings of Buddha. The man who was to become known as Buddha to the world was born as Prince Gautama of India but he rejected the worldly riches and abandoned the reigns of power when... Religion/History/Biographies Pages 170

The Complete Works of Guy de Maupassant *by Guy de Maupassant*   ISBN: *1-59462-157-8*   **$16.95**
"For days and days, nights and nights, I had dreamed of that first kiss which was to consecrate our engagement, and I knew not on what spot I should put my lips..."   Fiction/Classics Pages 240

The Art of Cross-Examination *by Francis L. Wellman*   ISBN: *1-59462-309-0*   **$26.95**
Written by a renowned trial lawyer, Wellman imparts his experience and uses case studies to explain how to use psychology to extract desired information through questioning   How-to/Science/Reference Pages 408

Answered or Unanswered? *by Louisa Vaughan*   ISBN: *1-59462-248-5*   **$10.95**
Miracles of Faith in China   Religion Pages 112

The Edinburgh Lectures on Mental Science (1909) *by Thomas*   ISBN: *1-59462-008-3*   **$11.95**
This book contains the substance of a course of lectures recently given by the writer in the Queen Street Hall, Edinburgh. Its purpose is to indicate the Natural Principles governing the relation between Mental Action and Material Conditions...   New Age/Psychology Pages 148

Ayesha *by H. Rider Haggard*   ISBN: *1-59462-301-5*   **$24.95**
Verily and indeed it is the unexpected that happens! Probably if there was one person upon the earth from whom the Editor of this, and of a certain previous history, did not expect to hear again...   Classics Pages 380

Ayala's Angel *by Anthony Trollope*   ISBN: *1-59462-352-X*   **$29.95**
The two girls were both pretty, but Lucy who was twenty-one who supposed to be simple and comparatively unattractive, whereas Ayala was credited, as her Bombwhat romantic name might show, with poetic charm and a taste for romance. Ayala when her father died was nineteen...   Fiction Pages 484

The American Commonwealth *by James Bryce*   ISBN: *1-59462-286-8*   **$34.45**
An interpretation of American democratic political theory. It examines political mechanics and society from the perspective of Scotsman James Bryce   Politics Pages 572

Stories of the Pilgrims *by Margaret P. Pumphrey*   ISBN: *1-59462-116-0*   **$17.95**
This book explores pilgrims religious oppression in England as well as their escape to Holland and eventual crossing to America on the Mayflower, and their early days in New England...   History Pages 268

QTY

The Fasting Cure *by Sinclair Upton*   ISBN: *1-59462-222-1*   **$13.95**
In the Cosmopolitan Magazine for May, 1910, and in the Contemporary Review (London) for April, 1910, I published an article dealing with my experi-
ences in fasting. I have written a great many magazine articles, but never one which attracted so much attention... New Age/Self Help/Health Pages 164

Hebrew Astrology *by Sepharial*   ISBN: *1-59462-308-2*   **$13.45**
In these days of advanced thinking it is a matter of common observation that we have left many of the old landmarks behind and that we are now pressing
forward to greater heights and to a wider horizon than that which represented the mind-content of our progenitors...   Astrology Pages 144

Thought Vibration or The Law of Attraction in the Thought World   ISBN: *1-59462-127-6*   **$12.95**

by William Walker Atkinson   *Psychology/Religion Pages 144*

Optimism *by Helen Keller*   ISBN: *1-59462-108-X*   **$15.95**
Helen Keller was blind, deaf, and mute since 19 months old, yet famously learned how to overcome these handicaps, communicate with the world, and
spread her lectures promoting optimism. An inspiring read for everyone...   *Biographies/Inspirational Pages 84*

Sara Crewe *by Frances Burnett*   ISBN: *1-59462-360-0*   **$9.45**
In the first place, Miss Minchin lived in London. Her home was a large, dull, tall one, in a large, dull square, where all the houses were alike, and all the
sparrows were alike, and where all the door-knockers made the same heavy sound...   *Childrens/Classic Pages 88*

The Autobiography of Benjamin Franklin *by Benjamin Franklin*   ISBN: *1-59462-135-7*   **$24.95**
The Autobiography of Benjamin Franklin has probably been more extensively read than any other American historical work, and no other book of its kind
has had such ups and downs of fortune. Franklin lived for many years in England, where he was agent...   *Biographies/History Pages 332*

Name	
Email	
Telephone	
Address	
City, State ZIP	

☐ **Credit Card**   ☐ **Check / Money Order**

Credit Card Number	
Expiration Date	
Signature	

Please Mail to: Book Jungle
PO Box 2226
Champaign, IL 61825
or Fax to: 630-214-0564

ORDERING INFORMATION
web: *www.bookjungle.com*
email: *sales@bookjungle.com*
fax: *630-214-0564*
mail: *Book Jungle PO Box 2226 Champaign, IL 61825*
or PayPal *to sales@bookjungle.com*

Please contact us for bulk discounts

DIRECT-ORDER TERMS

20% Discount if You Order
Two or More Books
Free Domestic Shipping!
Accepted: Master Card, Visa,
Discover, American Express